The Good Doctor

A NEW COMEDY WITH MUSIC

By Neil Simon

SAMUEL FRENCH, INC.

45 WEST 25TH STREET   NEW YORK 10010

7623 SUNSET BOULEVARD   HOLLYWOOD 90046

LONDON   TORONTO

SPECIAL TAPE RECORDING FOR
THE GOOD DOCTOR

Samuel French, Inc. can furnish amateurs a tape recording of the special music for this play. We can lend the tape for a period not exceeding four (4) weeks upon receipt of exact performance dates, a $25.00 deposit, $20.00 rental fee, and a music royalty fee of $20.00 for the first performance, and $10.00 for each additional performance thereafter, plus $3.00 to cover first-class postage and handling. Orders should be placed to allow one week for delivery, and *must* be accompanied by payment as mentioned. Tapes *must* be returned postpaid immediately after the production.

Stock royalty terms for the use of the tape quoted upon application.

Sheet music also available *for sale*: Price: $12.50, plus postage.

PLEASE NOTE: Use of this music in
productions is **mandatory.**

To Marsha

THE GOOD DOCTOR, by Neil Simon, directed by A. J. Antoon, music and orchestrations by Peter Link, lyrics by Neil Simon, scenery and costumes by Tony Walton, lighting by Tharon Musser, sound designed by Sandy Hacker, was presented by Emanuel Azenberg and Eugene V. Wolsk at the Eugene O'Neill Theatre, New York City, November 27th, 1973, with the following cast:

ACT ONE

THE WRITER ....Christopher Plummer
THE SNEEZE .... Christopher Plummer,
Rene Auberjonois, Marsha Mason, Barnard Hughes, Frances Sternhagen
THE GOVERNESS..Frances Sternhagen, Marsha Mason
SURGERY .....Christopher Plummer, Barnard Hughes
TOO LATE FOR HAPPINESS ....Barnard Hughes, Frances Sternhagen
THE SEDUCTION ....Christopher Plummer, Rene Auberjonois, Marsha Mason

Intermission—15 minutes

ACT TWO

THE DROWNED MAN ....Christopher Plummer, Rene Auberjonois, Barnard Hughes
THE AUDITION ..Christopher Plummer, Marsha Mason
A DEFENSELESS CREATURE ....Christopher Plummer, Barnard Hughes, Frances Sternhagen
THE ARRANGEMENT ....Christopher Plummer, Rene Auberjonois, Marsha Mason
THE WRITER ....Christopher Plummer
A QUIET WAR ....Christopher Plummer

5

The Concert

Oop Tymbali

Good Doctor Opus #1

Trans-Siberian Railroad

Father and Son

Good Doctor Opus #2

Morning Dance

Dance for Gathering 1

Dance for Gathering 2

The Concert precedes the play—walk off by Musicians into Scene 1

The Good Doctor

ACT ONE

Scene 1

"The Writer"

NARRATOR. . . . It's quite alright, you're not disturbing me. . . . I would much rather talk than work, yet here I am, day after day haunted by one thought, I must write, I must write, I must write. . . . This is my study, the room in which I write my stories. I built it myself, actually . . . cut the timber and fitted the logs. . . . Made an awful mess of it. . . . I do my writing here at the side of the room because the roof leaks directly over my desk. . . . I'd move the desk but it covers a hole I left in the floor. . . . And the floor was built on the side of the hill so in heavy rains, the room tends to slide downhill. . . . Many's the day I've stood in this cabin and passed my neighbors standing in the road. . . . Still, I'm happy here. . . . Although I don't get enough visitors to suit me. . . . People tend to shy away from writers. . . . They assume we're always busy thinking, not true. . . . Even my dear sweet Mother doesn't like to disturb me so she always tiptoes up here and leaves my food outside the door. . . . I haven't had a hot meal in years. . . . But I've done a good deal of writing in here. . . . Perhaps too much. . . . I look out the window and think that life is passing me at a furious rate. So, I ask myself the question . . . what force is it that compels me to write so incessantly, day after day, page after page, story after story. . . . And the answer is quite simple. . . . I have no choice. . . . I am a writer. . . . Sometimes I think I may be mad. . . . Oh, I'm quite harmless. . . . But I do admit to fits of wandering. . . . I'm engaged in conversations where I hear nothing and see only the silent movement of lips and answer a meaningless, "yes, yes, of course" and all the time I'm thinking, "He'll make a wonderful character for a story, this one." . . . Still, while I'm writing I enjoy it. And I like reading the proofs, but . . . as soon as it appears in print, I can't bear it. I see that it's all wrong, a mistake, that it ought never to have been written, and I am miserable. . . . Then the public reads it: "Yes, charming, clever. . . . Charming but a far cry from Tolstoy" . . . or "A fine thing, but Turgenev's 'Fathers and Sons' is better." . . . And so it will be to my dying day. . . . Charming and clever, charming and clever, nothing more . . . and when I die my friends will walk by my grave and say, "Here lies so and so, a good writer, but Turgenev was better." . . . It's funny, but before you came in, I was thinking to myself, perhaps I should give it up one day. . . . What would I do instead? . . . Well, I've never freely admitted this before, but to you here in the theatre tonight, I would like to tell you what I would most like to do with my life. . . . Ever since I was a small child, I always . . . I always . . . —excuse me a moment.—Just making a note. . . . An idea just occurred to me. A subject for a short story. . . . Hmm, yes, yes. . . . It was my mentioning the theatre that sparked me. . . . What were we talking about a moment ago. . . . No matter. My thoughts are consumed with this new story. . . . See if this appeals to you. . . . It starts in a theatre. [*Cue 1.*] . . . It starts on the opening night of the new season. [*Cue 2.*] . . . It starts [*Cue 3.*] with the arrival of all those dear and devoted patrons of the arts who wave and greet each other in the Grand Salon, commenting on how this one looks and how that one is dressed—scarcely knowing what play they are about to see that evening. [*Cue 3 out.*] . . . With the exception of one man . . . Ivan Ilyitch Cherdyakov! [*Cue 4.*]

(*The Theater Set appears.*)

ACT ONE

Scene 2

"The Sneeze"

NARRATOR. . . . If Ivan Ilyitch Cherdyakov, a civil servant, a clerk in the Ministry of Public Parks, had any passion in life at all, it was the theater. (*Enter* IVAN CHERDYAKOV *and his* WIFE. *He is in his mid-thirties, mild-mannered and unassuming. He and his* WIFE *are dressed in their best but certainly no match for the grandeur around them. They are clearly out of their element here. . . . They move into their seats. As his* WIFE *peruses her program* CHERDYAKOV *is beaming with happiness as he looks around and in back at the theater and its esteemed audience. . . . He is a happy man tonight. . . .*) . . . He certainly had hopes and ambitions for higher office and had dedicated his life to hard work, zeal and patience. . . . Still, he would not deny himself his one great pleasure. So he purchased two tickets in the very best section of the theater for the opening night performance of Rostov's "The Bearded Countess. . . . (*A splendidly uniformed* GENERAL *and his* WIFE *enter, looking for their seats.* . . .) . . . As fortune would have it, into the theater that night came His Respected Superior, General Mikhail Brassilhov, the Minister of Public Parks himself. [*Cue 4 out.*] . . . (*The* GENERAL *and his* WIFE *take their seats in the first row, the* GENERAL *being directly in front of* CHERDYAKOV.)

CHERDYAKOV. (*Leans over to* GENERAL.) . . . Good evening, General.

GENERAL. (*Turns, looks at* CHERDYAKOV *coldly.*)

Hmm? . . . What? Oh, yes. Yes. Good evening. (*The* GENERAL *turns front again, looks at his program.*)

CHERDYAKOV. Permit me, sir. I am Cherdyakov . . . Ivan Ilyitch. . . . This is a great honor for me, sir . . .

GENERAL. (*Turns, coldly.*) Yes.

CHERDYAKOV. . . . Like yourself, dear General, I too serve the Ministry of Public Parks. . . . That is to say, I serve *you,* who is indeed *himself* the Minister of Public Parks. . . . I am the Assistant Chief Clerk in the Department of Trees and Bushes.

GENERAL. Ahh, yes. . . . Keep up the good work. . . . Lovely trees and bushes this year. [*Cue 5.*] . . . Very nice. . . . (The GENERAL *turns,* CHERDYAKOV *sits back happy, grinning like a cat. The* GENERAL'S WIFE *whispers to him and he shrugs back. . . . Suddenly the unseen curtain rises on the play and they all applaud. . . . We hear either voices or music in the background. . . .* CHERDYAKOV *leans forward again.*)

CHERDYAKOV. My wife would like very much to say hello, General. . . . This is she. My wife . . . Madame Cherdyakov.

WIFE. (*Smiles.*) How do you do.

GENERAL. My pleasure.

WIFE. *My* pleasure, General.

GENERAL. How do you do. (*He turns front, flustered.* CHERDYAKOV *beams at his* WIFE . . . *then:*)

CHERDYAKOV. (*To* GENERAL'S WIFE.) Madame Brassilhov, my wife, Madame Cherdyakov.

WIFE. How do you do, Madame Brassilhov?

MADAME BRASSILHOV. (*Coldly.*) How do you do.

WIFE. I just had the pleasure of meeting your husband.

CHERDYAKOV. (*To* MADAME BRASSILHOV.) And I am my wife's husband. How do you do, Madame Brassilhov. (*The* NARRATOR *"Shushes" them.*)

GENERAL. (*To* NARRATOR.) Sorry. Terribly sorry. (*The* GENERAL *tries to control his anger as they all go back to watching the play. . . .*)

CHERDYAKOV. I hope you enjoy the play, sir.

GENERAL. I will if I can watch it. (*He is getting hot under the collar. They all go back to watching the performance.*)

NARRATOR. . . . Feeling quite pleased with himself for having made the most of this golden opportunity, Ivan Ilyitch Cherdyakov sat back to enjoy "The Bearded Countess." . . . He was no longer a stranger to the Minister of Public Parks. . . . They had become, if one wanted to be generous about the matter, familiar with each other. . . . And then, quite suddenly, without any warning, like a bolt from a gray thundering sky, Ivan Ilyitch Cherdyakov reared his head back—and

CHERDYAKOV. AHHHHHHHHH—CHOOOOOO-OOO!!! (CHERDYAKOV *unleashes a monstrous sneeze, his head snapping forward and the main blow of the sneeze discharges on the back of the* GENERAL'S *neck. The* GENERAL *winces and his hand immediately goes to his now-dampened neck.*) . . . Ohhh, my goodness, I'm *sorry*, your Excellency! I'm so terribly sorry! . . . (*The* GENERAL *takes out handkerchief and wipes his neck.*)

GENERAL. Never mind. It's alright.

CHERDYAKOV. *Alright?* . . . It certainly is *not* alright! It's unpardonable. It was monstrous of me. . . .

GENERAL. You make too much of the matter. Let it rest. (*He puts away his handkerchief.*)

CHERDYAKOV. (*Quickly takes out his own handkerchief.*) . . . How can I let it rest? . . . It was inexcusable. Permit me to wipe your neck, General. It's the least I can do. (*He starts to wipe the* GENERAL'S *neck. The* GENERAL *pushes his hand away.*)

GENERAL. Leave it be! It's alright, I say.

CHERDYAKOV. But I splattered you, sir. . . . Your complete head is splattered. . . . It was an accident, I assure you, but it's *disgusting!*

NARRATOR. Shhhh!

GENERAL. I'm sorry. My apologies.

CHERDYAKOV. . . . The thing is, your Excellency, it came completely without warning. . . . It was out of my nose before I could stifle it.

MADAME BRASSILHOV. Shhh!

CHERDYAKOV. Shh, yes, certainly. I'm sorry. . . . (*He sits back, nervously. He blows his nose with his handkerchief . . . then* CHERDYAKOV *leans forward.*) It's not a cold, if that's what you were worrying about, sir. Probably a particle of dust in the nostril. . . .

GENERAL. Shhh! (*They watch the play in silence . . . and* CHERDYAKOV *sits back unhappy with himself.*)

NARRATOR. . . . But try as he might, Cherdyakov could not put the incident out of his mind. . . . The sneeze, no more than an innocent anatomical accident, grew out of all proportions in his mind, until it resembled the angry roar of a cannon aimed squarely at the enemy camp. . . . He played the incident back in his mind, slowing the procedure down so he could view again in horror the infamous deed. [*Cue 6.*] (CHERDYAKOV, *in slow motion, repeats the sneeze again but slowed down so that it appears to us as one frame at a time. . . . It also seems to be three times as great in intensity as the original sneeze. The* GENERAL, *also in slow motion, reacts as though he has just taken a fifty-pound hammer blow at the base of his skull. . . . They all go with the slow motion of the "sneeze" until it is completed, when the Curtain falls and they all applaud. They all rise and begin to file out of the theater, chattering about the lovely evening they had just spent.*)

GENERAL. Charming. . . . Charming.

MADAME BRASSILHOV. Yes, charming.

GENERAL. Charming. . . . Simply charming. Wasn't it charming, my dear?

MADAME BRASSILHOV. I found it utterly charming. (CHERDYAKOV *stands behind them tapping the* GENERAL.)

NARRATOR. I was completely charmed by it.

CHERDYAKOV. (*Still tapping away at the* GENERAL.) Excuse me, Excellency—

GENERAL. Who's tapping? Somebody's tapping me. Who's that tapping?

CHERDYAKOV. I'm tapping, sir. I'm the tapper . . . Cherdyakov.

MADAME BRASSILHOV. (*Quickly pulls* GENERAL *back.*) Stand back, dear, it's the sneezer.

CHERDYAKOV. No, no, it's alright. I'm all sneezed out. . . . I was just concerned about your going out into the night air with a damp head.

GENERAL. Oh, that. It was a trifle. A mere faux pas. Forget it, young man. Amusing play, don't you think? Did you find it amusing?

CHERDYAKOV. Amusing? Oh, my goodness, yes. Ha, ha. So true. Ha, ha . . . I haven't laughed as much in years. . . . Ha ha ha. . . .

GENERAL. Which part interested you the most?

CHERDYAKOV. The sneeze. When I sneezed on you. . . . It was unforgivable, sir.

GENERAL. Forget it, young man. Come, my dear. It looks like rain. I don't want to get my head wet again.

MADAME BRASSILHOV. You shouldn't let people sneeze on you, dear. You're not to be sneezed at. (*They are gone.*)

CHERDYAKOV. I'm ruined! Ruined! . . . He'll have me fired from Trees and Bushes. . . . They'll send me down to Branches and Twigs.

WIFE. Come, Ivan.

CHERDYAKOV. What?

WIFE. You mustn't let it concern you. It was just a harmless little sneeze. The General's probably forgotten it already.

CHERDYAKOV. Do you really think so?

WIFE. No! I'm scared, Ivan. [*Cue 7.*]

NARRATOR. . . . And so they walked home in despair.

CHERDYAKOV. Perhaps I should send him a nice gift.
. . . Maybe some Turkish towels.

NARRATOR. Cherdyakov's once promising career had
literally been blown away. (*As they arrive home.*)

CHERDYAKOV. Why did this happen to me? Why did
I go to the theater at all. Why didn't I sit in the bal-
cony with people of our own class. They love sneezing
on each other.

WIFE. Come to bed, Ivan.

CHERDYAKOV. Perhaps if I were to call on the General and explain matters again, but in such a charming,
honest and self-effacing manner, he would have no
choice but to forgive me. . . .

WIFE. Maybe it's best not to remind him, Ivan.

CHERDYAKOV. No, no. If I ever expect to become a
gentleman, I must behave like one.

NARRATOR. And so the morning came. It so happened
this was the day the General listened to petitions . . .
and since there were fifty or sixty petitions ahead of
Cherdyakov, he waited from morning till late, late afternoon. . . . (CHERDYAKOV *crosses into set.*)

GENERAL. Next! . . . NEXT!

CHERDYAKOV. I'm not next, your Excellency . . .
I'm last.

GENERAL. Very well, then . . . Last!

CHERDYAKOV. That's me, sir.

GENERAL. Well, what is your petition?

CHERDYAKOV. I have no petition, sir. I'm not a peti-
tioner.

GENERAL. Then you waste my time.

CHERDYAKOV. Do you not recognize me, sir? We met
last night under rather "explosive" circumstances . . .
I am the splatterer.

GENERAL. The what?

CHERDYAKOV. The sneezer. The one who sneezed.
The sneezing splatterer.

GENERAL. Indeed? . . . And what is it you want
now? A Gezundheit?

CHERDYAKOV. No, Excellency . . . your forgiveness.
. . . I just wanted to point out there was no political
or anti-social motivation behind my sneeze. It was a
non-partisan, non-violent act of God. I curse the day the
protuberance formed itself on my face. It's a hateful
nose, sir, and I am not responsible for its indiscretions.
. . . (*Grabbing his own nose.*) Punish that which com-
mitted the crime, but absolve the innocent body behind
it. Exile my nose, but forgive me, your kindship . . .
forgive me. . . .

GENERAL. My dear young man, I'm not angry with
your nose. I'm too busy to have time for your nasal
problems. . . . I suggest you go home and take a hot
bath . . . or a cold one . . . take something . . . but
don't bother me with this silly business again. . . .
Gibber, gibber, gibber, that's all I've heard all day. . . .
(*Crossing off.*) Gibber, gibber, [*Cue 8.*] gibber, gibber
. . . (CHERDYAKOV *stands alone in the office sobbing.*)

CHERDYAKOV. Thank you, sir. . . . God bless you
and your wife and your household. . . . May your
days be sweet and may your nights be better than your
days. . . .

NARRATOR. The feeling of relief that came over
Cherdyakov was enormous. . . .

CHERDYAKOV. . . . May the birds sing in the morning at your window and may the coffee in your cup be
strong and hot. . . .

NARRATOR. . . . the weight of the burden that was
lifted was inestimable. . . .

CHERDYAKOV. (*Getting up.*) . . . I worship the chair
you sit on and the uniform you wear that sits on the
chair that I worship. . . .

NARRATOR. He walked home, singing and whistling
like a lark. . . . Life was surely a marvel, a joy, a
heavenly paradise. . . .

CHERDYAKOV. Oh, God, I am happy!!!

NARRATOR. And yet— [*Cue 8 out.*]

CHERDYAKOV. And yet—

NARRATOR. When he arrived home, he began to think . . .

CHERDYAKOV. Have I been the butt of a cruel and thoughtless joke?

NARRATOR. Had the Minister toyed with him?

CHERDYAKOV. If he had no intention of punishing me, why did he torment me so unmercifully?

NARRATOR. If the sneeze meant so little to the Minister, why did he deliberately cause Cherdyakov to writhe in his bed?

CHERDYAKOV. To twist in agony the entire night?

NARRATOR. Cherdyakov was furious!

CHERDYAKOV. I AM FURIOUS!!!

NARRATOR. He foamed and fumed and paced the night through and in the morning he called out to his wife . . . SONYA!

CHERDYAKOV. SONYA!! (*She rushes in.*) I have been humiliated.

WIFE. *You,* Ivan? Who would humiliate *you?* You're such a kind and generous person.

CHERDYAKOV. Who? I'll tell you who! . . . General Brassilhov, the Minister of Public Parks.

WIFE. What did he do?

CHERDYAKOV. The swine! I was humiliated in such subtle fashion, it was almost indiscernible. The man's cunning is equal only to his cruelty. He practically forced me to come to his office to grovel and beg on my knees . . . I was reduced to a gibbering idiot.

WIFE. You were that reduced?

CHERDYAKOV. I must go back and tell him what I think of him. The lower classes must speak up. . . . (*He is at the door.*) The world must be made safe so that men of all nations and creeds, regardless of color or religion, will be free to sneeze on their superiors! It is *he* who will be humiliated by *I!* [*Cue 9.*]

NARRATOR. And so, the next morning, Cherdyakov came to humiliate *he.* (*Light up on* GENERAL *at desk.*)

GENERAL. Last! (CHERDYAKOV *crosses to the* GEN-

ERAL'S *desk. He stands there glaring down at the* GEN-
ERAL *with a faint trace of a smile on his lips. The* GEN-
ERAL *looks up.*) Well?

CHERDYAKOV. (*Smiles.*) Well? . . . Well, you say?
. . . Do you not recognize me, your Excellency? . . .
Look at my face. . . . Yes. You're quite correct. It is
I once again.

GENERAL. (*Looks at him, puzzled.*) It is you once
again who?

CHERDYAKOV. (*Confidentially.*) Cherdyakov, Excellency . . . I have returned, having taken neither a hot
bath nor a cold one.

GENERAL. . . . Who let this filthy man in? . . .
What is it?

CHERDYAKOV. (*On top of the situation now.*) What
is it? . . . What is it, you ask? . . . You sit there behind your desk and ask, what is it? . . . You sit there
in your lofty position as General and Minister of Public Parks, a member in high standing among the upper
class and ask me, a lowly civil servant, what is it? . . .
You sit there with full knowledge that there is no equal-
ity in this life, that there are those of us who serve and
those that are served, those of us that obey and those
that are obeyed, those of us who bow and those that are
bowed to, that in this life certain events take place that
cause some of us to be humiliated and those that are
the cause of that humiliation . . . and still you ask,
"WHAT IS IT"!!!

GENERAL. (*Angrily.*) *What is it???* . . . Don't stand
there gibbering like an idiot! What is it you want?

CHERDYAKOV. *I'll tell you what I want!* I
wanted to apologize again for sneezing on you. . . . I
wasn't sure I made it clear. . . . It was an accident, an
accident, I assure you. . . .

GENERAL. (*Stands and screams out.*) *Out!* . . . *Out,
you idiot!!* . . . Fool! . . . Imbecile! . . . Get out of
my sight! I never want to see you again. . . . If you

ever cross my line of vision I'll have you exiled forever. . . . WHAT'S YOUR NAME??

CHERDYAKOV. Ch—Cherdyakov!

GENERAL. (*After second sneeze in office.*) . . . You germ spreader! . . . You maggot! . . . You insect! . . . You are lower than an insect. . . . You are the second cousin to a cockroach! . . . The son-in-law of a bed bug! . . . You are the nephew of *a ringworm!* . . . You are nothing, nothing, do you hear me? . . . *NOTHING!!!* [*Cue 10.*]

NARRATOR. . . . At that moment, something broke loose inside of Cherdyakov . . . something so deep and vital, so organic, that the damage that was done seemed irreparable. . . . Something drained from him that can only be described as the very life force itself. . . . (CHERDYAKOV *takes off his coat. He sits on the sofa, head in hands.*) . . . The matter was over, for once, for all, forever. [*Cue 11.*] . . . What happened next was quite simple. . . . (CHERDYAKOV *lies back on the sofa.*) . . . Ivan Ilyitch Cherdyakov arrived at home, removed his coat . . . lay down on the sofa—and died! [*Cue 11 out.*] (CHERDYAKOV's *head drops and his hand falls to the floor. . . . Blackout.*)

ACT ONE

Scene 3

"The Governess"

NARRATOR. (*Appears in a spot and addresses the audience.*) Wait! For those who are offended by life's cruelty, there is an alternate ending . . . "Ivan Ilyitch Cherdyakov went home, took off his coat, lay down on the sofa . . . and inherited five million rubles." . . . There's not much point to it, but it *is* uplifting. . . . I assure you it is not my intention to paint life any harsher than it is. . . . But some of us are indeed, trapped.

[*Cue 12.*] . . . Witness the predicament of a young governess who cares for and educates the children of a well-to-do family. (*Light up on the* MISTRESS *of the house at her desk. She has an account book in front of her.*)

MISTRESS. Julia!

NARRATOR. Trapped, indeed. . . .

MISTRESS. (*Calls again.*) Julia! (*A young governess,* JULIA, *comes rushing in* U. C. *She stops before the desk and curtsies.*)

JULIA. (*Head down.*) Yes, Madame?

MISTRESS. Look at me, child. Pick your head up. I like to see your eyes when I speak to you.

JULIA. (*Picks head up.*) Yes, Madame. (*But her head has a habit of slowly drifting down again.*)

MISTRESS. And how are the children coming along with their French lessons?

JULIA. They're very bright children, Madame.

MISTRESS. Eyes up. . . . They're bright, you say. Well, why not? . . . And mathematics? They're doing well in mathematics, I assume?

JULIA. Yes, Madame. Especially Vanya.

MISTRESS. Certainly. I knew it. I excelled in mathematics. . . . He gets that from his mother, wouldn't you say?

JULIA. Yes, Madame.

MISTRESS. Head up. . . . (*She picks head up.*) That's it. Don't be afraid to look people in the eyes, my dear. . . . If you think of yourself as inferior, that's exactly how people will treat you. . . .

JULIA. Yes, M'am.

MISTRESS. A quiet girl, aren't you? . . . Now then, let's settle our accounts. . . . I imagine you must need money although you never ask me for it yourself. . . . Let's see now, we agreed on thirty rubles a month, did we not?

JULIA. (*Surprised.*) Forty, M'am.

MISTRESS. No, no, thirty. I made a note of it. (*Points*

to book.) I always pay my governesses thirty. . . . Who told you forty?

JULIA. You did, M'am. I spoke to no one else concerning money. . . .

MISTRESS. Impossible. . . . Maybe you *thought* you heard forty when I said thirty. . . . If you kept your head up that would never happen. . . . Look at me again and I'll say it clearly . . . *Thirty rubles a month.*

JULIA. If you say so, M'am.

MISTRESS. Settled. Thirty a month it is. . . . Now then, you've been here two months exactly.

JULIA. Two months and five days.

MISTRESS. No, no. Exactly two months. I made a note of it. . . . You should keep books the way I do so there wouldn't be these discrepancies. . . . So—we have two months at thirty rubles a month, comes to sixty rubles. Correct?

JULIA. (*Curtsies.*) Yes, M'am. Thank you, M'am.

MISTRESS. Subtract nine Sundays . . . We did agree to subtract Sundays, didn't we?

JULIA. No, M'am.

MISTRESS. Eyes! Eyes! . . . Certainly we did. . . . I've always subtracted Sundays. I didn't bother making a note of it because I always do it. . . . Don't you recall when I said we will subtract Sundays?

JULIA. No, M'am.

MISTRESS. Think.

JULIA. (*Thinks.*) . . . No, M'am.

MISTRESS. You weren't thinking. Your eyes were wandering. . . . Look straight at my face and look hard. . . . Do you remember now?

JULIA. (*Softly.*) Yes, M'am.

MISTRESS. I didn't hear you, Julia.

JULIA. (*Louder.*) Yes, M'am.

MISTRESS. Good. I was sure you'd remember. . . . Plus three holidays. Correct?

JULIA. Two, M'am. Christmas and New Years.

MISTRESS. And your birthday. That's three.

JULIA. I worked on my birthday, M'am.

MISTRESS. You did? There was no need to. My governesses never worked on their birthdays. . . .

JULIA. But I did work, M'am.

MISTRESS. But that's not the question, Julia. We're discussing financial matters now. I will, however, only count two holidays if you insist. . . . Do you insist?

JULIA. I did work, M'am.

MISTRESS. Then you *do* insist.

JULIA. No, M'am.

MISTRESS. Very well . . . That's three holidays, therefore we take off twelve rubles. . . . Now then, four days little Kolya was sick and there were no lessons.

JULIA. But I gave lessons to Vanya.

MISTRESS. True. But I engaged you to teach two children, not one. Shall I pay you in full for doing only half the work?

JULIA. No, M'am.

MISTRESS. So we'll deduct it. . . . Now, three days you had a toothache and my husband gave you permission not to work after lunch. Correct?

JULIA. After four. I worked until four.

MISTRESS. (*Looks in book.*) I have here, "Did not work after lunch." . . . We have lunch at one and are finished at two, not at four, correct?

JULIA. Yes, M'am. But I—

MISTRESS. That's another seven rubles . . . Seven and twelve is nineteen . . . Subtract . . . that leaves . . . Forty-one rubles. . . . Correct?

JULIA. Yes, M'am. Thank you, M'am.

MISTRESS. Now then, on January fourth you broke a teacup and saucer, is that true?

JULIA. Just the saucer, M'am.

MISTRESS. What good is a teacup without a saucer, eh? . . . That's two rubles. . . . The saucer was an heirloom, it cost much more but let it go. I'm used to taking losses.

JULIA. Thank you, M'am.

MISTRESS. Now then, January ninth, Kolya climbed a tree and tore his jacket.

JULIA. I forbid him to do so, M'am.

MISTRESS. But he didn't listen, did he? . . . Ten rubles . . . January fourteenth, Vanya's shoes were stolen. . . .

JULIA. By the maid, M'am. You discharged her yourself.

MISTRESS. But you get paid good money to watch everything . . . I explained that in our first meeting. Perhaps you weren't listening. Were you listening that day, Julia, or was your head in the clouds?

JULIA. Yes, M'am.

MISTRESS. Yes, your head was in the clouds?

JULIA. No, M'am. I was listening.

MISTRESS. Good girl. So that means another five rubles off. (*Looks in book.*) . . . Ah yes . . . the sixteenth of January I gave you ten rubles.

JULIA. You didn't.

MISTRESS. But I made a note of it. Why would I make a note of it if I didn't give it to you?

JULIA. I don't know, M'am.

MISTRESS. That's not a satisfactory answer, Julia. . . . Why would I make a note of giving you ten rubles if I did not in fact give it to you, eh? . . . No answer? . . . Then I must have given it to you, mustn't I?

JULIA. Yes, M'am. If you say so, M'am.

MISTRESS. Well, certainly I say so. That's the point of this little talk. To clear these matters up. . . . Take 27 from 41, that leaves . . . fourteen, correct?

JULIA. Yes, M'am. (*She turns away, softly crying.*)

MISTRESS. What's this? Tears? Are you crying? . . . Has something made you unhappy, Julia? Please tell me. It pains me to see you like this. I'm so sensitive to tears. . . . What is it?

JULIA. Only once since I've been here have I ever

been given any money and that was by your husband. On my birthday he gave me three rubles.

MISTRESS. Really? There's no note of it in my book. I'll put it down now. . . . (*She writes in book.*) Three rubles . . . Thank you for telling me. . . . Sometimes I'm a little lax with my accounts. . . . Always short-changing myself. . . . So then, we take three more from fourteen, leaves eleven. . . . Do you wish to check my figures?

JULIA. There's no need to, M'am.

MISTRESS. Then we're all settled. Here's your salary for two months, dear. Eleven rubles. (*She puts pile of coins on desk.*) Count it.

JULIA. It's not necessary, M'am.

MISTRESS. Come, come. Let's keep the records straight. Count it.

JULIA. (*Reluctantly counts it.*) One, two, three, four, five, six, seven, eight, nine, ten . . . ? There's only ten, M'am.

MISTRESS. Are you sure? Possibly you dropped one. . . . Look on the floor, see if there's a coin there.

JULIA. I didn't drop any, M'am. I'm quite sure.

MISTRESS. Well, it's not here on my desk and I *know* I gave you eleven rubles. . . . Look on the floor.

JULIA. It's alright, M'am. Ten rubles will be fine.

MISTRESS. Well, keep the ten for now. And if we don't find it on the floor later, we'll discuss it again next month.

JULIA. Yes, M'am. Thank you, M'am. You're very kind, M'am. (*She curtsies and then starts to leave.*)

MISTRESS. Julia! (JULIA *stops, turns.*) Come back here. (*She crosses back to the desk and curtsies again.*) Why did you thank me?

JULIA. For the money, M'am.

MISTRESS. For the money? . . . But don't you realize what I've done? . . . I've cheated you . . . *robbed* you . . . I have no such notes in my book. . . . I made up whatever came into my mind. . . . Instead of

the eighty rubles which I owe you, I gave you only ten.
. . . I have actually stolen from you and still you thank
me. . . . Why?

JULIA. In the other places that I've worked, they
didn't give me anything at all.

MISTRESS. Then they cheated you even worse than I
did. . . . I was playing a little joke on you. A cruel
lesson just to teach you. You're much too trusting and
in this world that's very dangerous. . . . I'm going to
give you the entire eighty rubles. (*Hands her an en-
velope.*) It's already for you. The rest is in this en-
velope. Here, take it.

JULIA. As you wish, M'am. (*She curtsies and starts
to go again.*)

MISTRESS. Julia! (JULIA *stops.*) . . . Is it possible
to be so spineless? . . . Why don't you protest? Why
don't you speak up? Why don't you cry out against this
cruel and unjust treatment? . . . Is it really possible
to be so guileless, so innocent . . . such a—pardon me
for being so blunt—such a simpleton?

JULIA. (*The faintest trace of a smile on her lips.*)
. . . Yes, M'am . . . it's possible. [*Cue 13.*] (*She
curtsies again and runs off. . . . The* MISTRESS *looks
after her a moment, a look of complete bafflement on
her face. . . . The lights fade.*)

ACT ONE

Scene 4

"Surgery"

(*Light up on side of stage. The* NARRATOR.)

NARRATOR. Wait! [*Cue 13 out.*] For those again who
are offended by life's cruelty, there is an alternate ending . . . Julia was so enraged by such cruel and unjust
treatment—that she quit her job on the spot and went
back to her poor parents—where she inherited five mil-

lion rubles. . . . It is my intention someday to write a
book of 37 short stories—all with that same ending. I do
love it so. . . . You know that it has been said that
Man is the only living creature that is capable of laughter and it is that faculty that separates us from the
lower forms of life. . . . Yet, one must wonder about
this theory when we examine some of the objects of our
laughter. . . . For example, Pain. . . . Pain, needless
to say, is no laughing matter . . . unless of course, it's
someone else who is doing the suffering. . . . Why the
sight of a man in the throes of excruciating agony from
an abcessed tooth that has enlarged his jaw to the size
of an orange is funny, I couldn't say. . . . It is *not*
funny. . . . Not in the least. But in the village of
Astemko, [*Cue 14.*] where they have very little access
to entertainment, a man with a toothache can tickle their
ribs for weeks. . . . Certainly, Sergie Vonmiglasov, the
sexton, saw nothing humorous about it. . . . (*The
lights come up on the Surgery Room. . . . There is a
chair on one side and on the other is a table with various
medical instruments. . . . Enter the* SEXTON, VONMI-
GLASOV. . . . *He is a large, heavy-set man wearing a
cassock and a wide belt. He is a priest in the Russian
Church. A scarf is wrapped around his face and his jaw
is enlarged. He crosses the stage and moans in pain.*) Yet,
as he passed through the village on his way to the hos-
pital, his moans and groans won him more chuckles
than sympathetic remarks. Wouldn't they find it even
more amusing to know that the good doctor who nor-
mally performed the extractions of angry teeth was
away at the wedding of his daughter, and the duty fell
to his new assistant, Kuryatin, an eager medical stu-
dent, if, alas poor sexton, an inexperienced one. [*Cue
14 out. End of Tape No. 1.*] (*The* NARRATOR *during
this speech has changed into a not too clean doctor's
coat, lights a cigar stub and as the* SEXTON *enters the
door* KURYATIN, *the assistant, picks up a large, one-
word titled book: "Teeth."*)

SEXTON. Ohhh! . . . Ohhh!

KURYATIN. Ahh, greetings, Father. What brings you here?

SEXTON. The pain is unbearable. . . . It is beyond unbearable. . . . It is uendurable!

KURYATIN. Where exactly is the pain?

SEXTON. Where *isn't* it? Everywhere! It's not just the tooth. It's the whole side of my mouth.

KURYATIN. How long have you had this agony?

SEXTON. Ten years.

KURYATIN. *Ten years??*

SEXTON. Since yesterday morning it seems like ten years. . . . I must have sinned terribly to deserve this. God must have dropped *all* other business to punish me this way. . . . Where is the doctor?

KURYATIN. The doctor is away on personal business. He left the care of his patients in my young, capable hands.

SEXTON. But are you a doctor?

KURYATIN. In every way except a degree . . . I am a Doctor-to-be.

SEXTON. Then I'm a patient-to-be. Goodbye. (*He turns, then moans.*)

KURYATIN. (*Trying to stop him from leaving.*) I can assure you, the only thing that prevents me from being a called "Doctor" is the formality of an examination. . . . I'm skilled. I'm just not "titled." Please, I beg you for this opportunity. Please, sit in the chair, Father.

SEXTON. (*Crosses to chair.*) Heaven help me today. (*He sits.*) Oghhh . . . even sitting hurts.

KURYATIN. No doubt the nerves are inflamed. Once removed, the pain will cease to be.

SEXTON. You're going to remove the nerves?

KURYATIN. The tooth that's connected to the nerve . . . It's a simple matter of surgery. . . . (*Smoke is blown in the* SEXTON's *face.*)

SEXTON. The cigar!

KURYATIN. What?

SEXTON. Your cigar is burning my eyes. . . .

KURYATIN. I'm sorry. Would you rather I put it out? I only smoke it to steady my nerves.

SEXTON. Smoke it. Smoke the cigar.

KURYATIN. Thank you. . . . (*Starts to untie scarf. He can't untie it so he takes a large pair of scissors from his coat pocket, yanks the scarf and cuts it quickly. The* SEXTON *screams, "Aggghhhhhh!"*) There! . . . Now let's see what we have here.

SEXTON. (*Puts his hands up.*) I pray for you. I pray to the Saints and to our dear Lord in Heaven . . . be gentle with me . . . spare me pain.

KURYATIN. My dear Sexton . . . we are living in an age of advanced science. . . . In skilled hands, there is no longer need for pain. . . . If it's gentleness you want, it's gentleness you'll have. . . . Now, are you ready? (*The* SEXTON *nods.*) Good. . . . Now please open your mouth so I can examine you. . . . (*The* SEXTON *stiffens.*) . . . Come, come, open your mouth, please. . . . (*The* SEXTON *grips the chair, but won't open his mouth.*) . . . My dear Sexton . . . inexperienced as I am, I *know* it's essential you open your mouth. . . . It's mandatory to all work concerning the mouth to have it open first. . . . It would be highly impractical for me to pull your tooth from the *out*side. . . . Now please open up. (*The* SEXTON *opens his lips but his teeth remain clenched.*) . . . Not the lips, the entire mouth . . . I don't want to brush your teeth, I want to examine them. . . .

SEXTON. Will you be gentle?

KURYATIN. Didn't I promise you I would?

SEXTON. As a child I was promised many things I never got.

KURYATIN. There is no pain connected to this part. This part is merely an examination to find out what must be done, where and how. NOW OPEN UP!! (*The* SEXTON *opens his mouth.*) Good. . . . Now let's have a look. (KURYATIN *peers in. The* SEXTON *groans in pain.*) Ahh, yes. There it is. . . . There's the ugly little fellow. . . . You're a nasty one, aren't you?

SEXTON. Stop talking to it! Don't make friends with it, pull it out!

KURYATIN. Don't rush me, I'm evaluating. . . . Your tooth has a hole in it big enough to drive a horse and carriage through. . . . (*He gags at what he sees.*)

SEXTON. What is it?

KURYATIN. It's even disgusting to look at. . . . But if this is going to be my profession, I have to get used to these things. . . . Now then, I'm going to try something.

SEXTON. Be gentle.

KURYATIN. As though I were your own mother.

SEXTON. My mother didn't like me. Gentler.

KURYATIN. . . . I want to see how exposed the nerve is. . . . All I'm going to do is . . . *gently,* blow on your tooth. . . . That's all. . . . Alright? . . . Excuse me. (*He steps to one side and tests his breath on his hand.*) Here goes. (KURYATIN *puckers his lips and gently blows into the* SEXTON's *mouth. . . . The* scream *we hear is bloodcurdling.*) I have some information for you. . . . The nerve is exposed.

SEXTON. Is that how far science has advanced? Blowing on teeth?

KURYATIN. (*Crossing to instrument table.*) It's still inconclusive. More work must be done in this field. So much depends on the temperature of the doctor's breath. . . . Ahhh, here we are. (*He picks up a forceps.*)

SEXTON. What are you going to do with that?

KURYATIN. The tooth *has* to be pulled. It'll be out quicker than you can spit. (*He crosses back to chair.*)

SEXTON. (*He crosses himself.*) Oh, Merciful God . . .

KURYATIN. Surgery is nothing. It's all a matter of a firm hand. *Open up!*

SEXTON. (*Chants religioso.*) I pray for you. May the

Lord enlighten your soul. . . . May He give you health and quickness . . . mostly quickness.

KURYATIN. (*Sings.*) Aaahhh men.

SEXTON. (*Sings along.*) Aaahhh men. . . .

KURYATIN. (*Having gotten the* SEXTON *to open his mouth in song, he holds it firmly open.*) This will come out easily. . . . Some teeth give you trouble, I admit, but that's only when the roots are deep. . . . I hope you prayed for shallow roots. . . . Alright, here we go. (*He is just about to enter the* SEXTON'S *mouth when the* SEXTON *grabs his wrist.*) . . . Don't do that. . . . Don't grab my hand. . . . Let go. . . . Let go, I say. (*The* SEXTON *lets go . . . then* KURYATIN *starts to enter his mouth again when the* SEXTON *grabs his wrist once more.*) You've got my hand again. . . . If I'm going to pull your tooth I need my hand. . . . Now let go. (SEXTON *won't let go.*) . . . Are you going to let go of my hand? . . . If you don't let go of my hand, I'm going to take these forceps and pull your fingers out. . . . (*The* SEXTON *still won't let go so* KURYATIN *raps him on the knuckles with the forceps. He pulls his hand away in pain.*) . . . There! . . . Now let's try once more. . . . (*The* SEXTON *opens his mouth and* KURYATIN *places the forceps in his mouth.*) Good, good. . . . Don't twitch, sit still. . . . You're *twitching* again! . . . Now the important thing is to get a deep enough hold so we don't break the crown. . . .

SEXTON. Ohhh . . . Ohhhhhhhhh!

KURYATIN. (*He forces the* SEXTON'S *mouth open and inserts forceps again.*) Alright, this time I got a firm grip on the little monster. . . . Now whatever I do, don't grab my hands. . . . I'm going to have enough trouble with your tooth without *you* interfering. . . . Steady now. . . . When I say three . . . One . . . Two . . . THREE! (*And* KURYATIN *pulls . . . and pulls . . . and pulls. . . . The tooth will not give and the* SEXTON *begins to slide down in his chair. . . .* KURYATIN *keeps pulling and succeeds only in pulling*

the SEXTON *with him . . . not only down in his seat
. . . but clear out of it . . . onto the floor . . . across
the floor . . . to the other side of the room . . . and
then finally* yanks *it out as the* SEXTON *screams and
moans.*)

SEXTON. AAAAAAGGGGGGHHHHHHHHH-
HH!!!

KURYATIN. (*Falling to one side, victorious.*) Got it!
Got it! . . . I pulled it out! My first tooth!

SEXTON. You pulled it alright. . . . I hope they pull
you into the next world like that! . . . (*Feels face.*)

KURYATIN. (*Looks at forcepts.*) Oh, oh . . . I knew
it. The crown broke. . . . You've still got the roots in
your mouth. What a mess this is going to be. *I told you
not to twitch!*

SEXTON. (*Still lying on the floor.*) *You butcher! You
carpenter!* You're God's vengeance for my sins. . . .
Compared to *you,* the toothache was a joy!

KURYATIN. *You ignorant peasant!* The only thing
harder than the roots in your tooth are the brains in
your head. . . .(*He gets up and starts for the* SEX-
TON.) Now get back in the chair. We have unfinished
business.

SEXTON. (*Having gotten up, starts to back away
from him.*) . . . Keep away from me, Sorcerer! . . .
If you put your fingers in my mouth, it'll be the first
solid food I eat this week. (*The* SEXTON *bolts for the
door only to find* KURYATIN *has beaten him there and
is blocking his exit.*)

KURYATIN. You're not leaving here until those roots
come out. It's a question of professional pride. (*The*
SEXTON *dashes away from* KURYATIN. *Having gotten
him away from the door, the* SEXTON *runs back to the
door and near exhaustion they both finally collapse close
to each other . . . too tired to move.*)

SEXTON. I give up. . . .

KURYATIN. I failed in my duty.

SEXTON. Come, my son. Let us pray for a miracle.

(*The* SEXTON, *on his knees, crawls over to* KURYATIN *and helps him up on his knees. Then they both clasp their hands, look heavenward and pray. . . .*) Dear Lord in Heaven . . .

KURYATIN. Dear God above . . .

SEXTON. I plead for this good doctor . . .

KURYATIN. I pray for this poor creature . . . (*The lights begin to fade.*)

SEXTON. Keep his hand steady . . .

KURYATIN. Keep his mouth open . . . (*We are fading out.*)

SEXTON. Don't let him falter . . .

KURYATIN. Don't let him bite me . . .

SEXTON. Hail Mary!

KURYATIN. Hail Mary!

SEXTON. Hail Mary!

KURYATIN. Hail Mary!

SEXTON. Hail Mary!

KURYATIN. Hail Mary! [*Cue 1.*]

(*Blackout.*)

ACT ONE

Scene 5

"Too Late for Happiness"

(*A park. A* WOMAN, *in her early sixties, sits alone on a bench. She is reading a book. A* MAN, *in his early seventies, enters, carrying a walking stick and wears a hat and a large scarf around his neck. He tips his hat to her.*) [*Cue 1 out.*]

MAN. Good afternoon, Madame.

WOMAN. Good afternoon. (*She goes back to her book. . . . He takes a deep breath of the crisp fall air.*)

MAN. Ahhh . . . fine weather. . . . Fine weather indeed, wouldn't you say, Madame?

WOMAN. (*Looks up.*) I hadn't noticed really. . . . Yes, I suppose it is a lovely day. (*She goes back to her book.*)

MAN. Not many more of these left. . . . Winter's just beyond that tree there.

WOMAN. (*Closes her book, looks at sky.*) Mmm . . . The winters seem to be getting longer lately, have you noticed that? . . . They come sooner and stay longer.

MAN. I've noticed it, Madame. . . . Only in these last few years have I noticed it. (*The music comes in.......*)

WOMAN. (*Sings.*)
A KIND, GENTLE LOOKING PERSON
WHO'S SEEN HIS SHARE OF LIFE
A KIND, GENTLE LOOKING PERSON
AND HE'S NEVER WITH A WIFE.

IF THIS KIND, GENTLE LOOKING
   GENTLEMAN
SPEAKS ONCE AGAIN TO ME
SHOULD THIS SHY, NERVOUS WIDOWED
   LADY
GO OUT WITH HIM FOR TEA?

MAN. (*Sings.*)
A FINE FIGURE OF A LADY
WITH QUALITY AND TONE
A FINE FIGURE OF A LADY
AND SHE ALWAYS SITS ALONE.

SHOULD THIS FINE FIGURE OF A
   GENTLEMAN
WHO'S OLDER THAN THE SEA
ASK A FINE FIGURE OF A LADY
IF SHE'D LIKE TO SHARE SOME TEA?

(*Speaks.*) . . . I was wondering, Madame . . .

WOMAN. Yes?

MAN. I er . . . I was wondering . . . do you have the time of day?

WOMAN. I don't carry a timepiece.

MAN. Ahhh . . . No matter. . . . It wasn't urgent. . . . My business can wait. . . . Yes . . . it can wait. . . . (*Sings.*)

SHOULD THIS OLD WEATHER BEATEN GENTLEMAN
TAKE ONE MORE CHANCE AT LIFE
SHE REMINDS ME OF THAT SWEET LADY
WHOM I LOVINGLY CALLED WIFE.

WOMAN. (*Sings.*)

I HAD MY TENDER HEARTED GENTLE-MAN
CAN I GO THROUGH AGAIN
ALL THE PAIN, JOY AND ALL THE SORROW
THAT YOU GET FROM LOVING MEN.

BOTH.

IS IT TOO LATE FOR HAPPINESS
TOO LATE FOR FLINGS
TOO LATE TO ASK FOR LOVE
THERE AREN'T MANY SPRINGS
LEFT FOR
PEOPLE WHO SPEND THEIR NIGHTS
WAITING FOR THE DAY
FOR SOMEONE TO SHARE DELIGHTS
LONG SINCE PASSED AWAY.

TOO LATE FOR HAPPINESS
TOO SOON FOR FALL
TOO LATE FOR ANYTHING
ANYTHING AT ALL.

MAN. (*Looking up, speaks.*) . . . Seems to be clouding up a bit.

WOMAN. Yes . . . I'm beginning to feel a chill in the air.

MAN. Oh? . . . Would you like my scarf for your neck?

WOMAN. Thank you, no. . . . It's getting late. I should be getting home.

MAN. Yes, yes, of course . . . I was thinking the same thing . . . the same thing . . . unless—

WOMAN. . . . Yes?

MAN. Unless you would care to join me for tea? A cup of hot tea? . . . Might be just the right thing . . . a cup of tea. . . .

WOMAN. . . . Tea? . . . Tea, you say. . . . Well, that's very nice of you . . . I—I would love to. . . .

MAN. . . . You would?

WOMAN. Yes . . . but not today. . . . It's getting late. . . . Perhaps tomorrow.

MAN. Yes, yes, of course. . . . Perhaps tomorrow. . . . Good. . . . There's always tomorrow. . . .

WOMAN. Good day, sir.

MAN. Good day, Madame. . . .

BOTH. (*Sing.*)
YES, THERE'S STILL TIME FOR
    HAPPINESS
TIME TO BE GAY
STILL TIME TO ANSWER YES—
    (*Pause.*)
. . . BUT JUST NOT TODAY. . . .
(*They turn and walk off slowly as the music and lights fade.*)

ACT ONE

Scene 6

"The Seduction"

Lights up on the NARRATOR. *He is in suit and hat, pince nez and carrying his walking stick. He walks*

*to stage right. There is a small public garden. A
tree and a bench. He looks to the wings, as if waiting for someone, then out to the audience.*

NARRATOR. . . . Peter Semyonych was the greatest
seducer of other men's wives that I've ever met. . . .
He was successful with *all* women for that matter, but
there was a special challenge to beautiful women married to prominent, rich, successful men. . . . I could
never do him justice, let him tell you in his own words.
. . . (*He removes his glasses, puts them in his pocket,
clears his throat, assumes a more debonair posture and
becomes* PETER SMYONYCH.)
PETER. . . . If I may say so myself, I am the greatest seducer of other men's wives that I've ever met. . . .
I say this not boastfully, but as a matter of record. The
staggering figures speak for themselves. . . . For those
men interested in playing this highly satisfying but often
dangerous game, I urge you to take out pen and paper
and take notes. . . . I am going to explain my methods.
. . . In defense, married women may do likewise but it
will do them little good if they happen to be the chosen
victim. . . . My method has never failed. . . . Now
then, there are three vital characteristics needed. . . .
They are, patience, more patience and still more pa-
tence. . . . Those who do not have the strength to wait
and persist, I urge you to take up bicycling . . . row-
ing, perhaps. . . . Seducing isn't for you. . . . Now
then, in order to seduce a man's wife, you must, I repeat *must,* keep as far away from her as possible. . . .
Pay her practically no attention at all. . . . Ignore her
if you must. . . . We will get to her—through the *husband.* [*Cue 2.*] . . . (*He looks at his watch, then off
into wings.*) You are about to witness a practical dem-
onstration, for as it happens I am madly and deeply in
love this week. . . . My heart pounds with excitement
knowing that she will pass through this garden in a few
moments with her husband. Every fiber of my being tells

me to throw my arms around her and embrace her with all the passion in my heart. . . . But observe how a master works . . . I shall be cool almost to the point of freezing. . . . My heart of hearts and spouse, approaches. [*Cue 2 out.*] (*He turns the other way as the* HUSBAND *and his lovely, younger* BRIDE *approach taking an afternoon stroll in the park. She carries an umbrella to shade the afternoon sun.*)

HUSBAND. Ahh. Peter Semyonych, fancy meeting you here.

PETER. (*Doesn't look at* WIFE.) My dear Nikolaich, how good to see you. . . . You're looking well. (*To audience.*) Notice how I'm not looking at her.

HUSBAND. Thank you. And you, you gay devil, you're always looking well. . . . Excuse me, have you met my wife, Irena? . . . Of course, you have. . . . You sat next to her at dinner at the Vesnovs. . . . Irena, I don't know what this charmer said to you at dinner, but I must warn you that he is a scoundrel, a notorious bachelor and an exceptional swordsman. That's the best I can say for you, Peter.

PETER. You exaggerate, Nicky. (*Glances at the* WIFE.) Madame. Good to see you again. (*He doffs his hat but barely looks at her. She nods back, then turns and looks at the flowers.*)

HUSBAND. We were just taking a stroll. If you're not busy, why don't you walk with us?

PETER. That's very kind of you, Nikolaich, but as a matter of fact, I am rivieted to this spot. A new romance has just entered my life and my legs are like pillars of granite. . . . Until she is out of my sight, I will be incapable of movement. (*To audience.*) Too much do you think? As I said, be patient.

HUSBAND. Fantastic! You never cease to amaze me. Pretty, I suppose?

PETER. Suppose *magnificent*. Suppose *glorious* and you will suppose correctly.

HUSBAND. Any . . . "complications"?

PETER. As usual, a husband. I'm afraid my cause looks hopeless.

HUSBAND. Nonsense. I'm placing my money on you, Peter. And you know I never bet unless I'm sure of winning. Well, we're off. Good hunting, my boy. Good hunting. (*They start off.*)

PETER. (*Doffs his hat.*) Madame! (*Turns to audience.*) . . . Beautifully done, don't you think? . . . I'm sometimes awed by the work of a true professional. . . . Did you notice our eyes barely met, we exchanged hardly a word and yet how much she knows of me already. A) I am a popular bachelor, B) a man in love (always titillating to romantic women), C) a gifted sportsman (a nice contrast to her sedentary husband) and D) and this is most important, a dangerous man with the ladies. . . . Quite frankly, at this point she is disgusted by me . . . A) because I'm a braggart and a scoundrel, B) because I am shamelessly frank as to my intentions and C) because she thinks she's not the one I'm interested in. . . . Forgive me if I'm slightly overcome by my own deviousness. . . . By the way, are you getting all this down? It gets tricky from here on in. . . . Now then, next step, hypnosis . . . not hypnosis with your eyes, but with the poison of your tongue much like a venomous snake moving in for the kill . . . and what's more, the best channel is the husband himself. . . . Witness, as I "accidentally" run into him one day at the club. . . . (*He crosses to the "Club."* . . . *The* HUSBAND *is sitting reading a newspaper.* . . . PETER *takes up a newspaper and sits next to him. The* HUSBAND *looks up and notices him.*)

HUSBAND. . . . Peter . . . you're looking glum. . . . I take it your pursuit isn't going well. . . . (*He laughs.*)

PETER. Is it that obvious? . . . I'm doomed, Nicky. . . . I haven't seen her since last I met you and your dear wife. . . . I sleep little and eat less. I've had all my shirt collars taken in a half inch. Ah, Nicky, Nicky, why do I waste my valuable youth chasing women I can never truly call my own. . . . How I envy you.

HUSBAND. Me? . . . What's there about me that you envy?

PETER. Why, your marriage, of course. A charming woman, your wife let me tell you.

HUSBAND. Really? What is there about her that fascinates you so?

PETER. Her grace, her quiet charm, everything. But mostly it's the way she looks at you, Nicky. Oh, if only someone would look at me like that . . . with such adoring, loving eyes. It must send quivers through your body.

HUSBAND. Quivers? No, not really.

PETER. A tingle, perhaps? . . . Don't tell me you don't tingle when she looks at you.

HUSBAND. Of, of course. By all means. I tingle all the time.

PETER. She's an ideal woman, Nicky, believe that from a lonely bachelor and be glad fate gave you a wife like that.

HUSBAND. Perhaps fate will be as kind to *you*.

PETER. That's what I'm counting on. . . . Good heavens, I'm late for my doctor's appointment. (*He rises.*)

HUSBAND. What's he treating you for?

PETER. Melancholia. . . . Please say hello to your extraordinary wife but I urge you not to repeat our conversation. . . . It might embarrass her fragile sensitivities. . . . (*Sighs, as he walks away.*) Ahh, where oh where is the woman for me? (*Out of earshot of the* HUSBAND, *he stops and turns to audience . . . wicked smile.*) . . . I *know* where! . . . The question is: "How soon will she be mine?" [*Cue 3.*] . . . There is still work to be done . . . but not by me. . . . That task falls to my aide and accomplice. Oh, by the way, I saw Peter Semyonych today . . . (*Lights off on* PETER *and come up on the* HUSBAND *and the* WIFE *preparing for bed.*)

HUSBAND. . . . Oh, by the way, I saw Peter Semyonych today. . . . [*Cue 3 out.*]

WIFE. (*Putting up hair.*) Who?

HUSBAND. Peter Semyonych. The bachelor . . . we met him in the gardens last week. That attractive fellow . . . you remember.

WIFE. I remember what a loathsome man he is.

HUSBAND. You may not think so when you hear what he had to say about you.

WIFE. Nothing that braggart had to say would interest me.

HUSBAND. He spoke most enthusiastically about you. . . . He was enraptured by your grace, your quiet charm . . . and he seemed to feel that you were capable of loving a man in some extraordinary way. . . . It was something about your eyes and the way you looked so adoringly. . . . He certainly had a lot to say about you. . . . He went on and on . . . Well—good night, my dear.

WIFE. Good night. . . . . . . What else?

HUSBAND. Hmm?

WIFE. What else did he have to say about me?

HUSBAND. Peter?

WIFE. Whatever that loathsome man's name is. . . . What else did Peter Semyonych say about me?

HUSBAND. Well, that's more or less it. . . . What I told you.

WIFE. But you said he went on and on.

HUSBAND. He did.

WIFE. But you stopped. If he went on and on, don't stop. Either go on and on or let's go to bed.

HUSBAND. Well, he said how much he envied me. How much he wanted someone to look at him the way you look at me.

WIFE. How does he know how I look at you?

HUSBAND. Well, that day in the gardens. He must have been looking at you when you were looking at me. It sent a tingle through my whole body.

WIFE. The way I looked at you?

HUSBAND. Exactly, my precious.

WIFE. But you were looking at him. So you couldn't have seen how I was looking at you. As a matter of fact, I was looking at the flowers because he made m nervous the way he kept avoiding looking at me. . . . . You must have tingled for some other reason.

HUSBAND. It's getting rather confusing. . . . The point is, he found you fascinating. I thought it would please you.

WIFE. Well, it doesn't. . . . I would rather you didn't tell me such stories. . . . Are you planning to see him again soon?

HUSBAND. Tomorrow for lunch.

WIFE. . . . Well, I would rather not be discussed over lunch. . . . Tell him that. . . . And at dinner you can tell me what he said. . . . Good night, Nicky.

HUSBAND. Good night, my angel. (*Lights up on:*)

PETER. Good night, my love! (*To audience.*) I'm spellbound by my own powers. . . . I succeeded in not only piquing her interest, but causing her heart to flutter at the mention of my name, the same man she called loathsome not two minutes ago. . . . All this was accomplished, mind you, while I was home taking a pine-scented bath. . . . Luncheon the next day was not only nourishing, but productive. (*He crosses and sits with the* HUSBAND.) . . . By the way, old man, I ran into Nekrasov yesterday. The artist? . . . It seems he's been commissioned by some wealthy prince to paint the head of a typical Russian beauty. . . . He asked me to look out for a model for him. . . . I said I knew just the woman but I didn't dare ask her myself. . . . What do you think of asking your wife?

HUSBAND. Asking my wife what?

PETER. To be the model, of course. That lovely head of hers. It would be a damn shame if that exquisite face missed the chance to become immortalized for all the world . . .

HUSBAND. For all the world. Really? . . . Hmm . . . I see what you mean. . . .

PETER. Why don't you discuss it with her.

HUSBAND. Good idea. I'll discuss it with her. (*He gets up and crosses to the bedroom area. They are preparing for bed. To* WIFE.) Well, I said I would discuss it with you. What do you think?

WIFE. (*Brushing her hair.*) I think it's nonsense. . . . How did he put it to you? I mean, did he actually say "a typical Russian beauty"?

HUSBAND. Precisely. . . . And that it would be a damn shame if that exquisite face missed the chance to become immortalized for all the world. . . . That's exactly what he said.

WIFE. He gets carried away by his own voice. . . . Those *exact* words? You didn't leave anything out?

HUSBAND. Oh, yes . . . "That lovely face" . . . I left out "that lovely face." . . . He said that a number of times, I think. . . .

WIFE. He *does* go on, doesn't he? . . . How many times did he say it? Once? Twice? What?

HUSBAND. Let me think. It's hard to remember.

WIFE. It's not important . . . but in the future I wish you would write these things down. (*Blackout on them, light up on* PETER.)

PETER. (*To audience.*) . . . Have you seen me near her? . . . Have you heard me speak to her? . . . Has any correspondence passed between us? . . . No, my dear pupils. . . . And yet she *hangs* on my every word uttered by her husband. . . . Awesome, isn't it? . . . We apply this treatment from two to three weeks. . . . Her resistance is weakening, weakening, weakening. [*Cue 4.*] (*Back in bedroom.*)

HUSBAND. (*As usual, preparing for bed.*) I think his mind is elsewhere, if you ask me. . . . On some woman, from the looks of him.

WIFE. What woman? Has he mentioned any woman in particular?

HUSBAND. Oh, no. He's too discreet for that. He'll protect her good name at any cost. Instead, he talks of you all day. Poor fool, I'm beginning to feel sorry for him.

WIFE. It's really none of our concern, Nicky, did you ask him to dinner tomorrow? (*There was no break in that last speech.*)

HUSBAND. He's busy.

WIFE. The day after then.

HUSBAND. Busy.

WIFE. Next week. Next month. When? Doesn't the man eat?

HUSBAND. He says he's involved on a very important project and it will be months before he can see us. . . . He did say that with patience and persistence, good things will come to him. By the way, he thinks you should go on the stage.

WIFE. The stage? Me, on the stage? Why, in heaven's name?

HUSBAND. Well, he said—just a moment. I don't want to misquote him. (*He crosses to his jacket and takes a small notebook out.*)

WIFE. No, no. Take your time. Try to get it as accurately as possible.

HUSBAND. (*Reading.*) Ah, yes. He said, "with such an attractive appearance, such intelligence, sensitiveness, it's a sin for her to be just a housewife."

WIFE. (*Hand to her heart.*) Oh, dear, he said that?

HUSBAND. And that "ordinary demands don't exist for such women."

WIFE. Nicky, I don't think I want to hear anymore.

HUSBAND. "Natures like that should not be bound by time and space."

WIFE. Nicky, I implore you, please stop.

HUSBAND. And then he says, "If I weren't so busy, I'd take her away from you."

WIFE. He said that?

HUSBAND. Yes, right there. (*He points to notation.*)

WIFE. What did you say, Nicky? It's important I know what you said to him then.

HUSBAND. (*Laughs.*) Well, I said, "Take her, then. I'm not going to fight a duel over her." (*He laughs again.*)

WIFE. Nicky, you mustn't discuss me with him anymore. I beg you not to mention my name to him ever again.

HUSBAND. But I don't, my love. *He's* the one who always brings up the subject. . . . He actually accused me of not understanding you. . . . He shouted at me, "She's an exceptional creature, strong, seeking a way out. . . . If I were Turgenev, I would put her in a novel . . . 'The Passionate Angel' I would call it." . . . The man is weird. Definitely weird. (*The* WIFE *hangs her head disconsolately as we blackout on them and come up on* PETER.)

PETER. (*To audience.*) . . . He's delivering my love letters, sealing them with kisses and calls *me* weird . . . I ask you!! . . . So—let's see what we've got so far. The poor woman is definitely consumed with a passion to meet me. She is sure I am the only man who truly understands her. Her yawning, disinterested husband transmits my remarks but it is my voice she hears, my words that sing in her heart. . . . The sweet poison is doing its work. . . . I am relentless. . . . There is no room for mercy in the seducing business. . . . Observe how deftly the final stroke is administered. . . . For the faint-hearted, I urge you, look away! (*Light up on bedroom area. . . . They are eternally preparing for bed.*)

WIFE. *No*, Nicky! I don't want to hear. Not another word from him. Nothing.

HUSBAND. But exactly. That's what he said. He begged me to tell you *nothing*. He said he knew because of your sweet, sympathetic nature, you would worry to hear of someone else's distress.

WIFE. He's in distress?

HUSBAND. Worse . . . He's gloomy, morose, morbid, in the depths of despair.

WIFE. Oh, no . . . But why? What's the matter with him?

HUSBAND. Loneliness. . . . He says he has no relatives, no true friends, not a soul who understands him.

WIFE. But doesn't he know I . . . *we* understand him perfectly? . . . Doesn't he know how much I . . . *we* appreciate him and commune with him daily? . . . Doesn't he know how much I . . . we yearn to be with him? . . . You and I.

HUSBAND. I tried to make that clear. . . . I again urged him to come home to dinner with me. . . . But he said he can't face people. . . . He is so depressed he can't stay home. . . . He paces in the public garden where we met him, every night.

WIFE. What time?

HUSBAND. Between eight and nine. . . . By the way, we're invited to the Voskovecs tomorrow. Is eight o'clock alright for you?

WIFE. No, I'm visiting Aunt Sophia tomorrow. She's ill. I'll be there at nine . . . or a little after. (*Lights off bedroom and come up on gardens where* PETER *is strolling, waiting for his prey.*)

PETER. (*To audience.*) . . . Please, no applause . . . I couldn't have done it alone. . . . I share that honor with my good friend and collaborator, her husband. . . . He wooed her so successfully, that there is no carriage fast enough for her to be in my arms. . . . She ran all the way. [*Cue 5.*] . . . Observe! (*The* WIFE, *wearing a cloak, rushes in to the garden and then stops, breathless.*) . . . Now for the conclusion. . . . You *will* understand if I ask you to busy yourselves with your programs or such. These next few moments are private and I *am*, after all, a gentleman. [*Cue 5 out.*] (*He turns to* WIFE.) My dear . . . My sweet, dear angel . . . At last I can speak the words that I've longed—

WIFE. *No!* . . . Not a word! . . . Not a sound!
. . . Please . . . I couldn't bear it. . . . Not until
you've heard what's in my heart. (*She takes a moment
to compose herself.*) . . . For weeks now I've been in
torment. . . . You've used my husband as a clever and
devious device to arouse my passions . . . which I
freely admit, have been lying dormant these past seven
years. . . . Whether you are sincere or not, you have
awakened in me desires and longings I never dreamt
were possible. . . . You appeal to my vanity and I suc-
cumb. You bestir my thoughts of untold pleasures and
I weaken. You attack my every vulnerability and I sur-
render. I am here, Peter Semyonych, if you want me.
(*He starts to reach for her but she holds up her hand
for him to stop.*) But let me add this. I love my husband
dearly. He is not a passionate man, nor even remotely
romantic. Our life together reaches neither the heights
of ecstasy nor the depths of anguish. We have an *even*
marriage. Moderate and comfortable . . . and in ac-
cepting this condition and the full measure of his devoted love, I have been happy. . . . I come to you now
knowing that once you take me in your arms, my marriage and my life with Nicky will be destroyed for all
time. . . . I am too weak and too selfish to make the
choice . . . I rely on your strength of character. . . .
The option is yours, my dear Peter. . . . Whichever
one you choose will make me both miserable and eternally grateful. . . . I beg of you not to use me as an
amusement . . . although even with that knowledge, I
would not refuse you. I am yours to do as you will,
Peter Semyonych. . . . If you want me, open your
arms now and I will come to you. . . . If you love me,
turn your back and I will leave, and never see or speak
to you again. . . . The choice, my dearest, sweetest love
of my life is yours . . . I await your decision. (PETER
*looks at her, then turns his head and looks full face at
the audience. . . . He wants some advice but none is
coming. . . . He turns back to the* WIFE. *. . . He*

starts to raise his arms for her but they will not budge. It is as though they weighed ten tons each. . . . He struggles again with no results. He makes one final effort and then quickly changes his mind and turns his back on her.) . . . God bless you, Peter Semyonych . . . I wish life brings you the happiness you have just brought to me. (*She turns and runs off* U. L. PETER *then turns out to the audience . . . then reaches into his pocket, puts on his glasses and becomes the* NAR- RATOR *again . . . a little older and with none of the dash and charm of* PETER.)

NARRATOR. . . . Peter Semyonych, the *former* se- ducer of other men's wives, from that day on turned his attentions to single, unmarried women only. . . . Until one day, the perfect girl came along, and the con- firmed bachelor married at last. . . . (*He starts to walk off.*) . . . He is today a completely happy man . . . except possibly on those occasions when some dashing young officer tells him how attractive he finds his lovely young wife. [*Cue 6.*] . . . (*Dimout.*)

CURTAIN

INTERMISSION

ACT TWO

Scene 1

"The Drowned Man"

*Lights come up. . . . We are on a pier at the edge of a
dock. . . . It is dusk, a little foggy. . . . In the
harbor we can see some lights of distant ships. [Cue
7.] A foghorn bellows out at sea. . . . The NAR-
RATOR enters upstage L. with his walking stick. He
is wearing a great coat to keep out the evening
chill. . . .*

NARRATOR. (*Stops, looks out at sea . . . then turns
to the audience.*) . . . Just getting a little night air to
clear my mind. [*Cue 7 out.*] (*He takes a deep breath,
then exhales.*) . . . Ahhh, that's good . . . That's wonderful. . . . The sea air is so refreshing, it revitalizes
my entire body. . . . (*Another deep breath, exhales.*)
. . . But my mind is blocked . . . I have no thoughts,
no ideas . . . Most unusual for me. . . . Most times
they fill up my brain and overflow it like a cascading
fountain. . . . And tonight, nothing . . . And still I
have the urge to write. . . . Something will come, never
fear, always does. . . . These things happen to all men
in my profession at one time or another. . . . Writer's
block, we call it. . . . No need to panic, it'll pass soon.
. . . Wait! . . . Wait! . . . Hold on, an idea is coming.
. . . Yes. . . .Yes, aha. . . . Aha! . . . Terrible . . .
Bad idea. . . . False alarm. . . . Sorry I disturbed
you. . . Not only was it a bad idea, I've already written it. . . . It turned out awful. . . . This won't last
long. . . . It's just temporary. . . . However, it's get-

47

ting to be a very long 'temporary.' . . . Nothing is
coming. . . . My nerves are tightening. . . . Oh, God
help me. . . . No, no . . . I take that back. . . . I
mustn't rely on a collaboration with the Almighty. . . .
What selfishness. . . To ask God to take time out to
help me come up with an idea for a story. . . . Forgive
me, dear Lord. . . . I'll go home and try to sleep. . . .
Tomorrow is another day. . . . If, however, anything
does occur to you during the night, I would appreciate
it if you would make it known to me. . . . Even if it's
just the germ of an idea. . . . It doesn't have to be
original. . . . I'm very clever at twisting things around.
. . . Look how desperate I've become. . . . Asking the
Lord to resort to plagiarism for my petty needs. . . .
Home . . . I must get home and to bed before this
thing becomes serious. . . . (*He turns and starts to
walk off when a* FIGURE *appears in the shadows and calls
to him.*)

SAILOR. Psst! . . . You, sir. . . . Can I have a word
with you, sir?

NARRATOR. (*Turns and looks.*) Who's there? . . .
I can't see you in the dark. (*The* FIGURE *steps into the
light. His clothes are shoddy and he looks down on his
luck. He needs a shave, his gloves have only half fingers
and he smokes a cigarete butt.*)

SAILOR. 'Evening, sir. . . . I was wondering, sir, if
you might be in the mood for a little . . . er . . . "entertainment" this evening?

NARRATOR. (*Suspiciously.*) "Entertainment"? I'm
sure I don't know what you're talking about. (*He turns
away.*)

SAILOR. Sure you do, sir. . . . Entertainment . . .
Amusement, so to speak. . . . A little "diversion," if
you know what I mean.

NARRATOR. I think I *do* know what you mean and
I'm not interested. Go on, off with you. You should
know better than to make such a proposal to a gentleman.

SAILOR. You've never witnessed anything like *this* before, that I promise you. This is a once-in-a-lifetime offer. . . . Not even a *little* bit curious?

NARRATOR. Curiosity is the nature of my profession. But I try to keep it morally elevated. . . . Excuse me.

SAILOR. Perhaps you're right, sir. On second thought, this might be too much for a gentleman of your "sensitivities."

NARRATOR. (*Turns quickly.*) Wait!

SAILOR. (*Turns quickly.*) Got you with that last one, didn't I?

NARRATOR. I'm just asking, mind you . . . but er . . . just exactly what is this "entertainment" you speak of?

SAILOR. (*Moves closer, almost confidential.*) Well, sir . . . how would you like to see—a drowned man?

NARRATOR. (*Stares at him.*) . . . I beg your pardon?

SAILOR. A drowned man! . . . A man with his lungs filled up with salt water and stone dead from drowning. . . . How much would you pay to see that?

NARRATOR. *Pay?* . . *Pay* to see a drowned man? . . . Are you insane? . . . I wouldn't look at a drowned man if they paid *me*. . . . Why would I want to see a drowned man? . . . What's the point in looking at a man who drowned? . . . You're mad! Get out of here! (*He prods him away with his stick and starts to walk on, but the* SAILOR *runs around in front of him.*)

SAILOR. Three rubles, sir. That's all it'll cost you. Three rubles to see him first, before he's in the water, then in the agonizing act of drowning and then the grand finale, the man already drowned, rest his soul.

NARRATOR. What are you saying? That the man isn't drowned yet? That he's still alive and well?

SAILOR. Not only alive and well, but dry as a bone and standing before you. I'm the drowned man, sir.

NARRATOR. *You?* . . . You're going to drown yourself for three rubles? . . . You expect to charge me for your own suicide? . . . I must get away from this lunatic.

SAILOR. No, no, no, you've got it all wrong, sir. I don't actually drown. I *impersonate* a drowned man. I jump into the icy cold water, splash around a bit, flail my arms, yell for help a few times, go under, bubble, bubble, bubble, and then come up floating head down, all puffy like. It sends a chill up your spine. . . . Three rubles for individual performances, special rates for groups. Show starts in two minutes.

NARRATOR. I can't believe I'm actually discussing the price of admission to a drowning.

SAILOR. You miss the whole point, sir. This is not some sort of cheap thrill. It's a rich tableau filled with social implications. A drama, not tragic, but ironical, in view of its comic features.

NARRATOR. Comic? What's comic about it?

SAILOR. I blow up my cheeks and bulge my eyes out. Yell for help in a high squeaky voice. Sounds like a pig squealing. I'm the only one on the waterfront who can do it.

NARRATOR. Do you actually expect me to pay to hear an underwater pig squealer?

SAILOR. I've just had a very successful season, sir. Sold out in August. . . . What do you say, sir? Would you like me to book you now for the dinner show?

NARRATOR. What do you mean, dinner show?

SAILOR. I jump in, flail around and throw you a nice fish . . . I think the halibuts are running now, sir.

NARRATOR. Why do I stand here listening to this?

SAILOR. I wish you'd make up your mind soon, sir. In five minutes that restaurant throws its garbage in the water. Then it's messy. I have my pride.

NARRATOR. To hell with your pride. I doesn't prevent you from making a living imitating a deceased swimmer.

SAILOR. You sure know how to strike at a man's vulnerable points. That was cruel, sir.

NARRATOR. I'm sorry. I didn't mean to be cruel.

SAILOR. You completely overlook the finger points to my profession. . . . Look here, did you ever see a coal miner at the end of a day. Filth and grime all over his body. Soot up his nostrils and in his ears, black grit in his teeth. Disgusting. . . . Or a barber who goes home at night with the cuttings of other people's hair sticking to his hands. . . . I gets in his bread, in his soup, it's nauseating. . . . Do you know where a surgeon puts his fingers . . .

NARRATOR. Oh, please.

SAILOR. . . . or a farmer his feet? . . . Every man who works eventually touches something filthy. On the other hand, I deal with water. Water is wet, it's clean, it's purifying. . . . I don't have to take a bath when I come home at night. I've done it. . . . Can you say the same, sir?

NARRATOR. Do you think I'm going to discuss my toilet habits with you? My God you're infuriating. There must be a carriage around here. (*Calls out.*) Cabbie! Cabbie!

SAILOR. You'll regret it. You'll be back one night, bored to death, *dying* to see a good drowning and I'll be gone. This is my last week here. I close on Sunday. . . . Next week I'm in Yalta. (*A* POLICEMAN *strolls by in the background.*)

NARRATOR. There's a police officer. Now if you don't leave me alone, I'll have you arrested for soliciting.

SAILOR. I'm not soliciting. I'm in the Maritime Entertainment business.

NARRATOR. Drowning is not *maritime entertainment!* . . . You're a waterfront lunatic. *Officer! Officer!!*

SAILOR. (*Starting away.*) I'm going, I'm going . . . I'll tell you one thing, the drowning business isn't what it used to be. (*He runs off behind the pier. . . . The* POLICEMAN *walks quickly to the* NARRATOR.)

POLICEMAN. Can I help you, sir?

NARRATOR. There's a man there behind the docks.

There. He's been pestering me all evening. I shouldn't be surprised if he were deranged.

POLICEMAN. A lot of bad characters around these docks at night, sir. A gentleman like you shouldn't be wandering around here. . . . What was he pestering you about?

NARRATOR. Well, I'm warning you, you're going to find this strange. He wanted to charge me three rubles to watch him drown. Can you imagine? (*The* POLICE-MAN *looks at him strangely.*)

POLICEMAN. Strange? . . . It's outright thievery. It's not worth more than sixty kopecks. . . . You can get as fine a drowning as you'd want to see and not pay a penny more. Three rubles! What nerve!

NARRATOR. Officer, you seem to miss the point—

POLICEMAN. There's two brothers on the next pier, for one ruble each they'll give you a double drowning. . . . You have to know how to bargain with these men, sir. Get your money's worth.

NARRATOR. It's not a question of price.

POLICEMAN. Three rubles . . . Why the other day, right over there fourteen men acted out an entire *ship-*wreck for three rubles. . . . On a good day, for ten rubles you can get a *whole navy* going down. . . . Yes, sir. . . . Sixty kopecks, that's all *I'd* pay for a good drowning. . . . Stick to your price, sir, and have a nice evening. (POLICEMAN *tips his hat and walks off in the opposite direction. The* NARRATOR *stands there flabbergasted, not knowing what to do.* . . .)

NARRATOR. . . . It's come. . . . It's finally come. . . . The day the world has gone mad has arrived at last. (*The* SAILOR *emerges from his hiding place.*)

SAILOR. Psst! . . . Pssst! . . . I see the officer is gone. What did you tell him, sir?

NARRATOR. Tell him? I told him the truth . . . That you were mentally unbalanced. . . . Unfortunately he was a little more mentally unbalanced than you.

SAILOR. Still I appreciate your nòt causing me any

trouble, and in gratitude, I am reducing my price to an all-time low. Eighty kopecks.

NARRATOR. (*Furious.*) *Eighty?? Eighty, you thief!!* . . . You conniving, wretched, deceiving little thief, I won't pay you more than *sixty!*

SAILOR. *Sixty?* . . . Sixty kopecks for a drowning? . . . But where's my profit? . . . My *towels* cost me forty kopecks. . . . And another forty for the fella who fishes me out. . . . I'd be losing money on it. What's the point, I might as well stay under.

NARRATOR. You can't cheat me, sir. . . . Sixty kopecks for the drowning, take it or leave it.

SAILOR. (*Grumbly.*) . . . You're a hard man, sir. A hard man . . . Sixty kopecks it is. (*He sticks out his open hand for his money.*) . . . I pray to God my son doesn't want to be a drowner.

NARRRATOR. (*Counting out money.*) —thirty—forty —fifty—sixty. There's your money. . . . Now where shall I stand?

SAILOR. (*Pocketing money in a handkerchief.*) Right on the edge of the dock, sir. . . . Right up close, that's where you'll see all the action. (*He walks to edge of dock.*)

NARRATOR. It's a bit dark down there. . . . You're sure I'll be able to see well?

SAILOR. That's what make it so eerie. . . . The eerier, the more entertaining. . . . All the action's in the last ten seconds anyway. . . . Well, here I go. . . . Oh, I almost forgot. . . . When I come up for the third time, yell at the top of your lungs, *Popnichefsky! Popnichefsky!*

NARRATOR. Who's Popnichefsky?

SAILOR. He's the fellow who jumps in after me. I can't swim, sir.

NARRATOR. *You can't swim!* Are you trying to tell me you're going to drown without knowing how to swim?

SAILOR. That's what make it so exciting. Popnichef-

sky always waits till the very last second before jump-
ing in and pulling me out. He's in that restaurant, sir,
having a drink. Popnichefsky. Don't forget the name,
sir. . . . Well, I hope you enjoy the show. If you like
it, tell your friends. . . . In the soup, as we say. (*He
jumps in, yells for help.*) Help, help, I'm drowning
. . . I can't swim, help . . .

NARRATOR. Over here. A little towards me . . . I
can't see you too well there. . . .

SAILOR. Oh, God, help. Help, somebody, I'm drowning . . .

NARRATOR. Good . . . very good. . . . Yes, well,
that's enough of that . . . I don't want to see that part
anymore. . . . I don't have all night. . . . Can you
drown now . . .

SAILOR. Agggllllll . . .

NARRATOR. Do you hear me? . . . I would like to
have you drown now. . . . Where the devil is he? . . .
Ahh, there you are. . . . That's the third time, isn't it?
. . . Good heavens, what was that fellow's name?
[*Cue 8.*]

(*BLACKOUT*)

ACT TWO

Scene 2

"The Audition"

VOICE. (NARRATOR.) Next actress, please! [*Cue 8
out.*] Next actress, please! (*A young GIRL enters and
walks to the center of the stage. . . . She is quite nervous and clutches her purse for security. . . . She
doesn't know where to look or how to behave. This is
obviously her first audition. . . . She tries valiantly to
smile and give a good impression. . . . She has a handkerchief in her hand and constantly wipes her warm
brow.*) Name.

GIRL. (*Doesn't understand the question.*) What?

VOICE. Your name.

GIRL. Oh . . . Nina.

VOICE. . . . Nina? . . . Is that it? . . . Just Nina?

GIRL. Yes, sir . . . No, sir . . . Nina Mikhailovna Zarechnaya.

VOICE. . . . Age.

GIRL. My age?

VOICE. Yes, please . . . That means "How old are you"?

GIRL. (*Thinks.*) . . . How old are you looking for?

VOICE. Couldn't you answer the question simply, please?

GIRL. Yes, but I just wanted you to know, I can be any age you want . . . Sixteen, thirty. . . . In school I played a 78-year-old woman with rheumatism and everyone said it was very believable . . . a 79-year-old rheumatic woman told me so herself.

VOICE. Yes, but I'm not looking for a 78-year-old rheumatic woman . . . I'm looking for a 22-year-old girl. . . . Now how old are you?

GIRL. Twenty-two, sir.

VOICE. Really? . . . I would have guessed 27 or 28.

GIRL. I have a bad head cold, sir. It makes me look older. . . . Last year when I had influenza, the doctor thought I was 39. . . . I promise I can look 22 when you need it, sir. (*She wipes her forehead.*)

VOICE. Do you have a temperature?

GIRL. Yes, sir . . . a hundred and three.

VOICE. Good God, what are you doing walking around in the dead of winter with a hundred and three temperature? Go home, child. Go to bed. You can come back some other time.

GIRL. Oh, no, please, sir. I've waited six months to get this audition. I waited three months just to get on the six-month waiting list. . . . If they put me on the end of that list again, I'll have to wait another six months and by then I'll be 23 and it'll be too late to be

22. . . . Please let me read, sir. I'm really feeling much better. (*Feels forehead.*) I think I'm down to a-hundred-and-one now.

VOICE. I can see you have your heart set on being an actress.

GIRL. My heart, my soul, my very breath, the bones in my body, the blood in my veins—

VOICE. Yes, yes, we've had enough of you. medical history. . . . But what practical experience have you had?

GIRL. As what?

VOICE. Well, for example, the thing we're discussing. Acting. . . . How much acting experience have you had?

GIRL. . . . You mean on a stage?

VOICE. That's as good a place as any.

GIRL. Well, I studied acting for three years under Madame Zoblienska.

VOICE. She teaches here in Moscow?

GIRL. No. In my high school . . . In Odessa. . . . But she was a very great actress herself.

VOICE. Here in Moscow?

GIRL. No. In Odessa. . . .

VOICE. You are then, strictly speaking, an amateur.

GIRL. . . . Yes, sir . . . In Moscow. . . . In Odessa, I'm a professional.

VOICE. . . . Yes, that's all very well, but you see we need a 22-year-old professional actress in Moscow. . . . Odessa, although I grant you a lovely city, theatrically speaking, is not Moscow. . . . I would advise you to get more experience and take some aspirins. . . .

GIRL. (*Starts* R., *stops.*) I've traveled four days to get here, sir. . . . Won't you just hear me read?

VOICE. My dear child, I find this very embarrassing . . .

GIRL. Even if you did not employ me, just to read for you would be a memory I would cherish for all of my life. . . . If I may be so bold, sir, I think you are one of the greatest living authors in all of Russia. . . .

VOICE. Really? . . . That's very kind of you. . . . Perhaps we do have a *few* minutes—

GIRL. I've read almost everything you've written . . . The articles, the stories . . . (*She laughs.*) I loved the one about— (*She laughs harder.*) —the one about— (*She is hysterical.*) —oh, dear God, everytime I think of it, I can't control myself. . . .

VOICE. (*Laughs too.*) Really? Really? . . . Which story is that?

GIRL. (*Still laughing.*) —the "Death of a Government Clerk" . . . Oh, God, I laughed for days.

VOICE. "Death of a Govern—" . . . I don't remember that. . . . What was that about?

GIRL. Cherdyakov? . . . The sneeze . . . The sneezing splatterer? . . .

VOICE. Oh, yes. . . . You found that funny, did you? . . . Strange, I meant it to be sad. . . .

GIRL. Oh, it *was* sad. I cried for days. . . . It was tragically funny. . . .

VOICE. Was it, really? . . . And of everything you've read, what was your favorite?

GIRL. My *very* favorite?

VOICE. Yes, what was it?

GIRL. Tolstoy's "War and Peace." You asked me what my favorite was.

VOICE. . . . Well, you're an honest little thing, aren't you? . . . It's refreshing . . . Irritating, but refreshing. . . . Very well, what are you going to read for me?

GIRL. I should like to read from "The Three Sisters."

VOICE. Indeed? . . . Which sister?

GIRL. All of them . . . if you have the time.

VOICE. *All* of them? . . . Good heavens. Why don't you read the entire play while you're at it.

GIRL. Oh, thank you, sir . . . I know it all. . . . Act One . . . (*She looks up.*) . . . "A drawing room in the Prozorov's house. It is midday, a bright sun is shining through the large French doors . . ."

VOICE. *That's not necessary!!* . . . An excerpt will do nicely, thank you.

GIRL. Yes, sir . . . I would like to do the last moment of the play. . . .

VOICE. Good. Good. That shouldn't take too long. . . . Whenever you're ready.

GIRL. I've been ready for six months . . . Not counting the three months I waited to get on the six month waiting list.

VOICE. PLEASE, begin!

GIRL. Yes, sir. . . . (*She clears her throat, then just about to begin.*) . . . Oh, sir, could you please say, "Ta-ra-ra-boom-deay, sit on the curb I may" . . .

VOICE. Certainly not. Why would I say such an idiotic thing?

GIRL. I don't know, sir. You wrote it . . . Chebutykin says it at the end of the play. . . . It would help me greatly if you could read just that one line . . . I've waited six months, sir . . . I walked all the way from Odessa. . . .

VOICE. Alright, alright. . . . Very well, then . . . ready?

GIRL. Yes, sir.

VOICE. . . . "Ta-ra-ra-boom-de-ay, sit on the curb I may" . . .

GIRL. And Masha says, "Oh, listen to that music. They are leaving us. One has gone for good. Forever. We are left alone to begin our life over again. . . . We must live . . . we must live . . ." And Irina says, ". . . A time will come when everyone will know what all this is for . . . (*She is reading with more feeling and compassion than we expected.*) . . . why there is all this suffering, and there will be no mysteries, but meanwhile we must live . . . we must work, only work. . . . Tomorrow I shall go alone, and I shall teach in the school, and give my whole life to those who need it.

. . . Now it is autumn, soon winter will come and cover everything with snow, and I shall go on working, working . . ." . . . Shall I finish?

VOICE. (*Softly.*) Please.

GIRL. And Olga says, ". . . The music plays so gaily, so valiantly, one wants to live. Oh, my God. Time will pass, and we shall be gone forever . . . we'll be forgotten. Our faces will be forgotten, our voices, and how many there were of us, but our sufferings will turn into joy for those who live after us, happiness and peace will come to this earth, and then they will remember kindly and bless those who are living now. Oh, my dear sisters, it seems as if just a little more and we shall know why we live, why we suffer . . . If only we knew . . . If only we knew . . ." (*It is still.*) Thank you, sir. That's all I wanted. . . . You've made me very happy. . . . God bless you, sir. (*She walks off the stage. . . . The stage is empty.*)

VOICE. (*Softly.*) . . . Will someone go get her before she walks all the way back to Odessa. [*Cue 9.*]

(*DIMOUT*)

ACT TWO

Scene 3

"A Defenseless Creature"

Light up on an office of a bank official, KISTUNOV. . . . He enters on a crutch, his right foot is heavily encased in bandages, swelling it to three times its normal size. He suffers from the gout and is very careful of any mishap which would only intensify his pain. He makes it to his desk and sits. . . . An ASSISTANT, *rather harried, enters.* [*Cue 9 out.*]

ASSISTANT. (*With volume.*) Good morning, Mr. Kistunov!

KISTUNOV.   Shhh! . . . Please . . . Please   lower your voice.

ASSISTANT. (*Whispers.*) I'm sorry, sir.

KISTUNOV. It's just that my gout is acting up again and my nerves are like little firecrackers . . . The least little friction can send them off. . . .

ASSISTANT. It must be *very* painful, sir.

KISTUNOV. Combing my hair this morning was agony.

ASSISTANT. Mr. Kistunov . . .

KISTUNOV. What is it, Pochatkin?

ASSISTANT. There's a woman who insists on seeing you. . . . We can't make head or tail out of her story but she insists on seeing the directing manager. Perhaps if you're not well—

KISTUNOV. No, no. The business of the bank comes before my minor physical ailments. . . . Show her in, please . . . quietly. (*The* ASSISTANT *tiptoes out. A* WOMAN *enters. She is in her late forties, poorly dressed. She is of the working class. She crosses to the desk, a forlorn look on her face. . . . She twists her bag nervously.*) Good morning, Madame. Forgive me for not standing, but I am somewhat incapacitated. . . . Please sit down.

WOMAN. Thank you. (*She sits.*)

KISTUNOV. Now . . . what can I do for you?

WOMAN. You can help me, sir . . . I pray to God you can help. . . . No one else in this world seems to care. . . . (*And she begins to cry . . . which in turn becomes a wail . . . the kind of wail that melts the spine of strong men. . . .* KISTUNOV *winces and grits his teeth in pain as he grips the arms of his chair.*)

KISTUNOV. Calm yourself, Madame . . . I *beg* of you. . . . Please calm yourself. . . .

WOMAN. I'm sorry. (*She tries to calm down.*)

KISTUNOV. I'm sure we can sort it all out if we approach the problem sensibly and quietly. . . . Now what exactly is the trouble?

WOMAN. Well, sir . . . it's my husband . . . Collegiate Assessor Schukin. . . . He's been sick for five months . . . Five agonizing months. . . .

KISTUNOV. I know the horrors of illness and can sympathize with you, Madame. What's the nature of his illness?

WOMAN. It's a nervous disorder. . . . Everything grates on his nerves. . . . If you so much as touch him he'll scream out— (*And without warning, she* screams *a loud bloodcurdling scream that sends* KISTUNOV *almost out of his seat.*) . . . How or why he got it, nobody knows. . . .

KISTUNOV. (*Trying to regain his composure.*) I have an inkling. . . . Please go on, a little less descriptively, if possible.

WOMAN. Well . . . while the poor man was lying in bed—

KISTUNOV. (*Braces himself.*) You're not going to scream again, are you?

WOMAN. Not that I don't have cause . . . while he was lying in bed these five months, recuperating, he was dismissed from his job . . . for no reason at all.

KUSTINOV. That's a pity, certainly . . . but I don't quite see the connection with our bank, Madame. . . .

WOMAN. You don't know how I suffered during his illness . . . I nursed him from morning till night . . . Doctored him from night till morning . . . Besides cleaning my house, taking care of my children, feeding our dog, our cat, our goat, my sister's bird who was sick . . .

KISTUNOV. The bird was sick?

WOMAN. My *sister!* . . . She gets dizzy spells . . . She's been dizzy a month now . . . And she's getting dizzier every day. . . .

KISTUNOV. Extraordinary . . . However—

WOMAN. I had to take care of *her* children and *her* house and *her* cat and *her* goat and then her bird bit one of my children and so our cat bit her bird so my oldest daughter, the one with the broken arm, drowned my sister's cat and now my sister wants my goat in exchange or else she says she'll either drown my cat or break my oldest daughter's other arm. . . .

KISTUNOV. Yes, well, you've certainly had your pack of troubles, haven't you? . . . But I don't quite see—

WOMAN. And then, when I went to get my husband's pay, they deducted 24 rubles and 36 kopecks. For what, I asked? Because, they said, he borrowed it from the employees' fund . . . But that's impossible. He could never borrow without my approval. I'd break his arm . . . Not while he was sick, of course . . . I don't have the strength . . . I'm not well myself, sir . . . I have this racking cough that's a terrible thing to hear. . . . (*She coughs rackingly . . . so rackingly that* KISTUNOV *is about to crack.*)

KISTUNOV. . . . I can well understand why your husband took five months to recuperate . . . But what is it you want from me, Madame?

WOMAN. What rightfully belongs to my husband . . . His 24 rubles and 36 kopecks. . . . They won't give it to me because I'm a woman, weak and defenseless. . . . Some of them have laughed in my face, sir . . . *Laughed!* (*She laughs loud and painfully.* KISTUNOV *clenches everything.*) . . . Where's the humor, I wonder, in a poor, defenseless creature like myself? (*She sobs.*)

KISTUNOV. . . . None . . . I see none at all. . . . However, Madame, I don't wish to be unkind, but I'm afraid you've come to the wrong place. . . . Your petition, no matter how justified, has nothing to do with us. . . . You'll have to go to the agency where your husband was employed.

WOMAN. *What do you mean??* . . . I've been to *five* agencies already and none of them will even *listen* to my petition. . . . I'm about to lose my mind . . . The hair is coming out of my head. (*She pulls out a hand-*

ful.) Look at my hair. By the fistful. (*She throws a fistful on his desk.*) *Don't tell me to go another agency!!*

KISTUNOV. (*Delicately and disgustedly, he picks up her fistful of hair and hands it back to her. . . . She sticks it back in her hair.*) Please, Madame, keep your hair in its proper place. Now listen to me carefully. This-is-a-bank . . . A bank! We're in the banking business. We bank money . . . Funds that are brought here are banked by us. . . . Do you understand what I'm saying?

WOMAN. . . . What are you saying?

KISTUNOV. I'm saying that I can't help you.

WOMAN. Are you saying you can't help me?

KISTUNOV. (*Sighs deeply.*) I'm trying. I don't think I'm making headway.

WOMAN. Are you saying you can't believe my husband is sick? Here! Here is a doctor's certificate. (*She puts it on the desk and pounds it.*) There's the proof. Do you still doubt that my husband is suffering from a nervous disorder?

KISTUNOV. Not only do I not doubt it, I would *swear* to it.

WOMAN. *Look at it!* You didn't look at it!

KISTUNOV. It's really not necessary. I know *full well* how your husband must be suffering.

WOMAN. *What's the point in a doctor's certificate if you don't look at it?!* LOOK AT IT!!!

KISTUNOV. (*Frightened, quickly looks at it.*) Oh, yes . . . I see your husband is sick. . . . It's right here on the doctor's certificate. . . . Well, you certainly have a good case, Madame, but I'm afraid *you've still come to the wrong place.* (*Getting perplexed.*) I'm getting excited.

WOMAN. (*Stares at him.*) . . . You lied to me. . . . I took you as a man of your word and you lied to me.

KISTUNOV. I?? LIE?? . . . WHEN???

WOMAN. When you said you read the doctor's certificate. . . . You couldn't have . . . You couldn't have read the description of my husband's illness without seeing he was fired unjustly. . . . (*She puts certificate back on desk.*) Don't take advantage of me just because I'm a weak, defenseless woman. Do me the simple courtesy of reading the doctor's certificate. That's all I ask. Read it and then I'll go.

KISTUNOV. But I *read it!* What's the point in reading something twice when I've already *read it once.*

WOMAN. You didn't read it carefully.

KISTUNOV. I read it *in detail!*

WOMAN. Then you read it too fast. Read it slower.

KISTUNOV. *I don't have to read it slower. I'm a fast reader.*

WOMAN. Maybe you didn't absorb it. Let it sink in this time.

KISTUNOV. (*Almost apoplectic.*) I *absorbed* it! It *sank* in! I could pass a *test* on what's written here, *but it doesn't make any difference because it has nothing to do with our bank!*

WOMAN. (*She throws herself on him from behind.*) Did you read the part where it says he has a nervous disorder? Read that part again and see if I'm wrong.

KISTUNOV. THAT PART? OH, YES! I SEE YOUR HUSBAND HAS A NERVOUS DISORDER. . . . MY, MY . . . HOW TERRIBLE . . . *ONLY I CAN'T HELP YOU. . . . NOW PLEASE GO!* (*He falls back into his chair, exhausted.*)

WOMAN. (*Crosses to where his foot is resting.*) I'm sorry, Excellency. I hope I haven't caused you any pain.

KISTUNOV. (*Trying to stop her.*) Please, don't kiss my foot. (*He is too late—she has given his foot a most ardent embrace. He screams in pain.*) Aggghhh! . . Can't you get this into your balding head? . . . If you would just realize that to come to us with this kind of a claim is as strange as your trying to get a haircut in a butcher shop.

WOMAN. You can't get a haircut in a butcher shop.

. . . Why would anyone go to a butcher shop for a haircut. . . . Are you laughing at me?

KISTUNOV. *Laughing!* I'm lucky I'm breathing . . . Pochatkin.

WOMAN. Did I tell you I'm fasting? . . . I haven't eaten in three days. I want to eat but nothing stays down. . . . I had the same cup of coffee three times today.

KISTUNOV. (*With his last burst of energy, screams.*) *POCHATKIN!!*

WOMAN. I'm skin and bones . . . I faint at the least provocation. . . . Watch. (*She swoons to the floor.*) Did you see? You saw how I just fainted? Eight times a day that happens. . . . (POCHATKIN *finally rushes in.*)

POCHATKIN. What is it, Mr. Kistunov? What's wrong?

KISTUNOV. (*Screams.*) GET HER OUT OF HERE! . . . Who let her in my office?

POCHATKIN. You did, sir. . . . I asked you and you said, "Show her in."

KISTUNOV. I thought you meant a human being, not a lunatic with a doctor's certificate.

WOMAN. (*To* POCHATKIN.) He wouldn't even read it. . . . I gave it to him, he threw it back in my face. . . . You look like a kind person. Have pity on me. *You* read it and see if my husband is sick or not. (*She forces the certificate on* POCHATKIN.)

POCHATKIN. I *read* it, Madame. Twice!

KISTUNOV. Me, too. I had to read it twice, too.

POCHATKIN. You just showed it to me outside. You showed it to *every*one. We *all* read it. Even the doorman.

WOMAN. You just looked at it. You didn't read it.

KISTUNOV. Don't argue. Read it, Pochatkin. For God's sake, read it so we can get her out of here.

POCHATKIN. (*Quickly scans it.*) Oh, yes. It says your husband is sick. (*He looks up, gives it back to her.*) Now will you please leave, Madame, or I will have to get someone to remove you.

KISTUNOV. Yes! Yes! Good! Remove her! Get the doorman and two of the guards. Be careful, she's strong as an ox.

WOMAN. (*To* KISTUNOV.) If you touch me, I'll scream so loud they'll hear it all over the city. You'll lose all your depositors. No one will come to a bank where they beat weak, defenseless women. . . . I think I'm going to faint again. . . .

KISTUNOV. (*Rising.*) WEAK?? . . . DEFENSE-LESS?? . . . You are as defenseless as a charging rhinoceros! . . . You are as weak as the King of the Jungle! . . . You are a plague, Madame! . . . A plague that wipes out all that crosses your path. . . . You are a raging river that washes out bridges and stately homes. . . . You are a wind that blows villages over mountains. . . . It is women like you who drive men like me to the condition of husbands like yours.

WOMAN. Are you saying you're not going to help me?

KISTUNOV. Hit her, Pochatkin! Strike her! I give you permission to knock her down. Beat some sense into her!

WOMAN. (*To* POCHATKIN.) You hear? You hear how I'm abused? He would have you hit an orphaned mother. Did you hear me cough? Listen to this cough. (*She "racks" up another coughing spell.*)

POCHATKIN. Madame, if we can discuss this in my office— (*He takes her arm.*)

WOMAN. Get your hands off me. . . . Help! Help! I'm being beaten . . . Oh, merciful God, they're beating me.

POCHATKIN. I am not beating you. I am just holding your arm.

KISTUNOV. Beat her, you fool. Kick her while you've got the chance. We'll never get her out of here. . . .

Knock her senseless! (*He tries to kick her, misses and falls to floor.*)

WOMAN. (*Pointing an evil finger at* KISTUNOV . . . *she jumps on desk.*) A curse! A curse on your bank! I put a curse on you and your depositors! May the money in your vaults turn to potatoes . . . May the gold in your cellars turn to onions . . . May your rubles turn to radishes, and your kopecks to pickles. . . .

KISTUNOV. STOP! . . . Stop it, I beg of you. . . . Pochatkin, give her the money . . . Give her what she wants . . . Give her anything only get her out of here.

WOMAN. (*To* POCHATKIN.) 24 rubles and 36 kopecks . . . Not a penny more. . . . That's all that's due me and that's all I want. . . .

POCHATKIN. Come with me, I'll get you your money. (*He exits.*)

WOMAN. And another ruble to get me home. I'd walk but I have very weak ankles. (*She leans on* POCHATKIN.)

KISTUNOV. Give her enough for a taxi, anything, only get her out.

WOMAN. God bless you, sir. You're a kind man. I remove the curse. (*With gesture.*) Curse be gone! Onions to money, potatoes to gold—

KISTUNOV. (*Pulls on head.*) REMOVE HERRRR! Oh, God, my hair is falling out! (*He pulls some hair out.*)

WOMAN. Oh, there's one other thing, sir. I'll need a letter of recommendation so my husband can get another job. Don't bother yourself about it today. I'll be back in the morning. God bless you, sir. . . . (*She leaves.*)

KISTUNOV. She's coming back . . . She's coming back. . . . (*He slowly begins to go mad and takes stick or cane and begins to beat his bandaged leg.*) She's coming back . . . she's coming back. [*Cue 10.*]

(*DIMOUT*)

ACT TWO

Scene 4

"The Arrangement"

The lights come up. . . . We are on a wharf. . . . The
NARRATOR *enters and addresses the audience.*

NARRATOR. . . . This one goes back a good many
years ago to my youth . . . I was 19 years old to be
exact . . . and in the ways of love. I was not only un-
schooled, I hadn't even been in the classroom. . . . I
was so innocent and shy, that I actually thought that
since the beginning of time, no woman had *ever* been
completely unclothed. . . . As for connubial bliss, I
dared not think of it. . . . And as for impregnation, I
chose to believe it was caused by the husband giving the
wife a most ardent handshake before retiring ，. . . and
let it go at that. . . . But my father was a wonderful
man . . . quite liberal in his thinking and on the occa-
sion of my 19th birthday, he decided to introduce me
to the mysteries of love. . . . He was, however, a fru-
gal man, and decided to escort me himself, to see, in the
matter or bargaining, that I would not be taken advantage of. . . . Picture me, if you will, as my own dear
father . . . Antosha! . . . Antosha! Where are you?
. . . Don't stand there in the dark shaking like a puppy
dog. Come here. . . . We have some adolescence to get
over with. . . . (*Young* ANTON *appears, 19 years old,
as nervous as a puppy. He frets with his hat in his
hand.*)

BOY. I'm not well, Father. I'm sick.

FATHER. Sick? Sick? . . . What's wrong with you?

BOY. I haven't thought of it yet. Give me a few
minutes.

FATHER. Fear. That's all it is. Pubescent fear . . .
I was the same way when I was your age.

BOY. I never knew you were my age . . . I always thought of you as older.

FATHER. How old do you think I was when I was with my first woman?

BOY. You were with a woman, Father?

FATHER. Certainly, I was with a woman. All men who become fathers have been with a woman at some point in their life.

BOY. . . . The same woman?

FATHER. (*Yells.*) Certainly not the same woman. . . . My God, don't you ever discuss these matters with your young friends?

BOY. Oh, yes. . . . All the time. But we get too excited to listen.

FATHER. It's a man's obligation to enter a marriage experienced in the ways of love . . . otherwise valuable years are wasted in endless groping.

BOY. I don't mind wasting a few years groping, Father.

FATHER. It's all in the process of becoming a man, Antosha. First you learned to walk, then you learned to talk—and now it's time to learn this.

BOY. Are you sure, Father? I'm really not walking and talking that well.

FATHER. (*Irritated.*) . . . Antosha, we can't afford to delay any longer. I don't want you becoming an old man waiting to become a young man. . . . Now are you going to walk in there and have your first experience with a woman or do I have to punish you?

BOY. Father . . . I don't think we're going to find any women of high moral character around here.

FATHER. We're not looking for *high moraled* women. There are too damn many high moraled women in the world as it is. . . . That's why so many high moraled men have to come down to places like this. . . . Now let's get on with this business.

BOY. Can I hold your hand, Father?

FATHER. *Certainly not!* You can't go in there to become a man holding your father's hand. . . . Antosha, we don't have all day. . . . Your mother is expecting us home by 9 o'clock. . . . Now we have exactly an hour and ten minutes for you to mature.

BOY. You mean you told Mother where we were going?

FATHER. Do you think I'm so insensitive? I told her we were going out for a walk just to get some night air.

BOY. Won't she become suspicious when she notices that I've come home all grown up?

FATHER. It doesn't show, Anton. . . . You don't get spots like measles. . . . You may possibly have a small smile on your face, that's all. . . . Now come along.

BOY. Father . . . aren't there other ways to become a man? . . . I mean, couldn't I grow a moustache?

FATHER. Antosha, tell me the truth, if you'd rather not go through with it, I'll take you home. . . .

BOY. (*Nods.*) Take me home!

FATHER. *Wait till I ask the question!* Would you rather not go through with it? I'll take you home?

BOY. Take me home!

FATHER. I see! Very well, let's go home. . . . You can get in your tub and play with your sail boats until you're ready.

BOY. Will you be angry with me?

FATHER. No.

BOY. Will you be disappointed with me?

FATHER. No.

BOY. Will you be proud of me?

FATHER. No.

BOY. Alright, I'll do it.

FATHER. Good boy, Antosha.

BOY. . . . If I like it, can we do it again?

FATHER. No! . . . I didn't bring you down here with the intention of leaving you here. . . . By God, it's a difficult business being a liberal father. (*The* GIRL *enters.*)

GIRL. Evening, gentlemen!

BOY. Oh, God.

FATHER. Steady, boy, steady.

BOY. Is she . . . is she one of the teachers?

FATHER. She looks like the principal to me. . . . We're in luck, son. She's a charming looking girl. . . . I'll go over and attend to your tuition. . . .

BOY. Father . . . couldn't I take a correspondence course?

FATHER. No! Stand there! Don't move! . . . I'll be right back . . . and don't twiddle with your hat. . . . This is not hat twiddling business. . . . (*He crosses to* GIRL.) Good evening, Madame. . . . A lovely April night, wouldn't you say?

GIRL. Is it April already? . . . I don't get out very much.

FATHER. No, I can well understand that. . . . It's er . . . it's been a long time since I've been involved in such matters, but I would like to discuss with you a subject of some delicacy.

GIRL. 30 Rubles!

FATHER. So much for the delicacy . . . 30 Rubles you say. . . . Well, speaking for myself, I would say 30 Rubles was quite fair. . . . But it's not for me. It's for my young, inexperienced son. That's him! The one with the knees buckling.

GIRL. It's still 30 Rubles, sir. We don't have children's prices down here.

FATHER. No, of course not. . . . But 30 Rubles does seem a bit high for a boy of 19. . . . Would you consider 15 Rubles?

GIRL. For 15 Rubles I read Peter Rabbitt. Sir, a Norwegian ship is due in here tonight and I have to go in and put on my blonde wig.

FATHER. Wait! . . . There *is* an extenuating circumstance. . . . It's the boy's birthday and I wanted to give him a nice gift . . . what do you say?

GIRL. How about an umbrella?

FATHER. See here. In my day 30 years ago, I shared

the pleasures of the most delightful girl on this street
. . . Ilka the Milkmaid she was called, and she cost me
a mere 10 Rubles.

GIRL. Well, she's still here, if you want her she's
down to six Rubles now.

FATHER. Certainly not, good heavens . . .

BOY. Father? . . . Oh, Father?

FATHER. Yes?

BOY. Am I ready yet?

FATHER. In a minute . . . I'm still shopping. . . .
(*To* GIRL.) He's really a lovely boy . . . fragile and
sweet. . . . Tells the most delightful stories. . . . I'm
sure you'll find him most entertaining.

GIRL. Haven't you got it the wrong way around, sir?

BOY. Father, I'm getting chilly.

FATHER. (*To son.*) Well, run around, jump up and
down. Be patient. You've waited 19 years, it's just another few minutes. . . . (*To* GIRL.) 20 Rubles . . .
not a Kopeck more. . . . There's just so much I'm will-
ing to spend on education. Please, it's for my boy.

GIRL. (*Looks at him, then smiles.*) Settled! . . .
You're a good and loving father, sir, and I respect you
for it. . . . If I had a father like you I would never
have ended here on the streets bargaining with fathers
like you.

FATHER. (*Puzzled.*) I'm sure there's a moral in there
somewhere, I just don't see it yet. . . . Settled for 20
Rubles. . . . (*Gives her money.*) . . . Oh, there's just
one other request I have. . . . At the conclusion of the
evening's festivities, I would appreciate it greatly if you
would just say, "Happy Birthday from Poppa."

GIRL. (*Nods.*) "Happy Birthday from Poppa." . . .
Would you like any candles, sir?

FATHER. That's not necessary. Just be gentle and
kind to him. . . . Gentleness, that's all I ask. . . .
(*Wipes his eye.*) Good heavens, a tear. . . . What a
thing to cry over. . . .

GIRL. I'll wait upstairs . . . two flights up, second door on the left. . . . I'll be gentle, sir.

FATHER. Thank you. The girls nowadays seem to be so much more understanding.

GIRL. May I say, it's men like you who make me proud to serve in my profession.

FATHER. . . . What a wonderful nurse she would have made. . . . Antosha, school's in. (*He turns, crosses to* BOY.) Settled, my boy . . . 20 Rubles. . . . You have to know how to bargain with these people. . . . Well, off you go . . . two flights up, second door on the left. . . . I'll wait out here. Don't rush. (*The* BOY *starts, then stops.*)

BOY. Father, do I say anything to her?

FATHER. Like what?

BOY. Like "Hello"?

FATHER. "Hello" would be nice . . . "Goodbye" would be good too. . . . Go on, she's waiting.

BOY. Are there any "instructions" you want to give me?

FATHER. That's what I'm paying *her* good money for. . . . The questions you ask. . . . Go on, boy . . . before I have to pay her overtime.

BOY. Yes father . . . I'm going . . . I'm going . . . (*He stops.*)

FATHER. What is it now?

BOY. It's funny, but when I come down those stairs and out into the street . . . I won't be your little Antosha anymore . . . I'll be Anton the Man. . . . Thank you, Father. Well, goodbye. (*He gets to the door.*)

FATHER. Wait! (ANTON *stops.*) . . . Wait—Antosha!

BOY. What is it, Father?

FATHER. . . . I was just thinking . . . wouldn't you rather have a nice umbrella? . . . There's plenty of time next year to become a man. . . . Plenty of time next year. . . .

BOY. If you wish, Poppa. Yes, Poppa. [*Cue 11.*]

(The FATHER *puts his arm around the shoulder of the* BOY *and they turn and walk off into the night. . . . Music plays as the stage dims out.)* [*Cue 11 out.*]

ACT TWO

Scene 5

"The Writer"

The lights come up and the NARRATOR *comes downstage carrying his "Portfolio" of writings.*

NARRATOR. . . . I hope that portrait of my father came out with some affection. I loved him very much. . . . And yet with him, as with all the other characters I've shared with you tonight, I have a sense of betrayal. . . . When I put down my pen at the end of a day's work, I cannot help but feel that I have robbed my friends of their precious life fluid. . . . What makes my conscience torment me even more, is that I've had a wonderful time writing today . . . but before I go . . . what was it we were talking about? Early on, before the story of Cherdyakov? . . . Ahh, yes . . . I was about to say what it was, as a child, I most wanted to do with my life. Well, then— (*He thinks for a moment.*) Funny, for the life of me I can't remember . . . but somehow, as I stand here with a feeling of great peace and contentment, in some measure I suspect I must be doing it. Thank you for this visit. If ever you pass this way again, please drop in. Good night. . . . Wait! . . . There's an alternative ending. . . . If ever you pass this way again, I hope you inherit five million rubles. Good night. [*Cue 12.*] (*He turns and moves upstage.*)

CURTAIN

PRODUCTION NOTE: The following material was added by Mister Simon which wasn't included in the first printing (similar) as in the original broadway production.

ACT TWO

Scene 6

"A Quiet War"

Light up on a park bench, a small tree behind it. The NARRATOR *enters carrying a walking stick and crosses to bench and sits. He is enjoying the afternoon air.*

NARRATOR. . . . In the vicinity of Veshenko Square there is a small park that is seldom crowded. Here and there a pair of young lovers strolling; a mother teaching her young child to take its first brave steps, the inevitable failures cushioned on the soft, green grass; a dog owner throwing a stick for his faithful friend to fetch, which he does faithfully and interminably; a young girl calling out "Fresh Flowers for sale," which is only partly true; they're for sale but they are not terribly fresh. . . . Still, it's a rather lovely, peaceful and quiet setting. . . . Certainly one would never suspect this charming little spot would soon turn into a battlefield . . . which it did with marked regularity each Tuesday afternoon at three. . . . It was a quiet war. No guns, no booming cannons, no marching feet . . . but nonetheless a war. . . . The adversaries were two aged and retired officers, one military, the other naval. . . . They had served their country long and with distinction and now, in

the twilight of their lives, still had flickerings of sparks
igniting their passions, if alas, no fire was ever started.
. . . They debated on every subject under the sun;
whores, politics, women, literature . . . they never
seemed to run out of subjects to disagree about . . .
and they never did agree on anything except to meet
again the following Tuesday at three on the same bench
for the purpose of continuing their disagreements. . . .
(*A church bell in the distance chimes three times. The*
NARRATOR *takes out his pocket watch and checks it.*)
. . . We are fortunate. Today is Tuesday and the time
you've just heard. . . . I'd best move on because the
bench I am sitting on is the field of battle and I have
no wish to get caught in the crossfire . . . (*He gets*
up, starts to cross left . . .) I will watch from a safe
vantage point— (*Pointing off with can.*) —there, near
the children's swing. . . . Approaching from the east
comes the Army . . . from the west, the Navy. . . .
If I had a drum, I would roll it. . . . (*He exits. . . .*
A few seconds later, from the opposite side comes the
retired ARMY OFFICER. *He is in civilian clothes, a*
long top coat, quite old and bent. He carries a cane
and uses it. His white hair is covered by a fur hat.
. . . *He crosses to the bench and sits on one side. . . .*
From the opposite side, the retired NAVAL OFFICER *ap-*
proaches. He is equally old and bent, with white hair,
a cane and similarly dressed . . . he crosses to the
same bench and sits. The two men do not give any
indication of greeting each other. They sit silently,
staring ahead, leaning on their canes, licking their
lips. Finally.)

ARMY. . . . Cool weather we're having today.

NAVY. . . . It's warmer than yesterday. (*Pause.*)

ARMY. They say it may rain.

NAVY. (*Looks up, squints.*) Here comes the sun.
. . . It's coming. (*Pause.*)

ARMY. Soooo. . . . It's your turn. Pick a subject.

NAVY. (*Thinks.*) . . . I've got one.

ARMY. A good one?

NAVY. (*Nods.*) In my opinion.

ARMY. Alright. . . . What's the subject?

NAVY. (*Pauses.*) . . . Lunch!

ARMY. (*Thinks, then turns and looks at him for the first time.*) . . . Lunch? . . . Your subject is lunch?

NAVY. It's my turn, isn't it? . . . I pick lunch.

ARMY. (*Shrugs.*) Not much of a subject, in my opinion.

NAVY. Does that mean you concede?

ARMY. I concede nothing. . . . I merely stated it's a poor subject. . . . But I accept the challenge. If it's lunch, it's lunch. . . . Start.

NAVY. Are you ready?

ARMY. Would I say "Start" if I weren't ready? . . . "Start" means I'm ready. Go ahead. . . . Start!

NAVY. Very well. . . . Appetizers! . . .

ARMY. (*Agreeing.*) Appetizers, right.

NAVY. To start off a good lunch, the best appetizer is herring.

ARMY. Wrong.

NAVY. Wrong? Herring is not the best appetizer?

ARMY. It's good. I didn't say it wasn't good. But not as good as caviar.

NAVY. You're wrong. . . . Caviar is too rich for an appetizer. . . . It's a dish that should be reserved for special occasions . . . with a little champagne . . . A snack, yes. An appetizer. Never.

ARMY. Are you telling me that fresh caviar, lemon juice, finely chopped eggs, raw onions, garnished with parsley and served on lightly salted wafer thin bisquits is not a good appetizer?

NAVY. Do you want to compare it with herring in white cream sauce, marinated onions, two large black olives sitting on either end of the plate, sprinkled with dill and the end piece of fresh baked brown bread to soak up the drippings of the herring, the onion, and the dill into one final succulent mouthful? Heh?

ARMY. (*Thinks.*) . . . You argue well. . . . I concede the appetizer.

NAVY. Thank you. . . . Let's move on to the soup.

ARMY. I don't think we'll have any argument here. . . . Borscht!

NAVY. Borscht? . . . For soup you pick borscht? Out of all the soups in God's creation, you pick an ordinary dish of borscht?

ARMY. Not in a dish. In a bowl. And there is nothing ordinary about piping hot borscht prepared with sweet sugar beets. . . . Ukranian style—with ham and country sausages . . . and topped with a thick, white sour cream. . . . Are you prepared to challenge a soup like that?

NAVY. I would sooner have Cabbage soup steaming from the pot with thick chunks of boiled potatoes and globs of tender meat still hanging from the bone. . . . And sooner than Cabbage soup, I would take a full bodied vegetable soup . . . with carrots, with fresh asparagus, with cauliflower stalks, with parsnips and ripe tomatoes . . . and sooner than vegetable soup, I would take a fish soup, with tripe and giblets and young kidneys floating on the top so thick you would have to *push* your way into the soup. . . .

ARMY. Wait a minute, wait a minute. . . . I'm not talking about your run of the mill ordinary every day served in a restaurant borscht. . . . I'm talking about *peasant* borscht! . . . The kind you eat with a pound of hot corn bread in your left hand and in your right hand, a thick . . . heavy . . . wooden spoon.

NAVY. . . . A wooden spoon? . . . That's different. . . . You didn't mention a wooden spoon before. . . . I concede the soup.

ARMY. Accepted.

NAVY. How do we stand?

ARMY. You won the appetizer, I won the soup.

NAVY. Up to here, it's a very close lunch. . . . Next course.

ARMY. Next course is fish.

NAVY. Fish? . . . Oh. Well, we can forget about the fish. I don't care for fish. . . . Whatever you choose for fish is fine with me.

ARMY. You don't like fish?

NAVY. I'm not dead set *against* it. . . . It's alright once in a great, great while. . . . It's not substantial enough. . . . It never satisfies me. . . . To me the important part of the meal is the roast. . . . Why don't you pick out a fish and then we can move on to the roast.

ARMY. So you concede the fish?

NAVY. (*Nods.*) Mention a fish and I'll concede it.

ARMY. Pike. A nice piece of Pike.

NAVY. Carp is better.

ARMY. (*Angry.*) You just conceded the fish!

NAVY. I didn't know you were going to say Pike. . . . I don't find Pike a tasty fish.

ARMY. A nice Pike fried in brown butter with stewed tomatoes and a thick mushroom sauce? That's not tasty?

NAVY. It's tasty if you smother it with Carp broiled in lemon juice.

ARMY. But you already conceded the fish.

NAVY. Alright. I won't make an issue of it . . Change it to Carp and I'll concede the fish.

ARMY. But Carp is *your* fish. Then *I'd* be conceding.

NAVY. You could have chosen Carp ahead of me. The option was yours.

ARMY. Will you concede if I drop Pike and pick another fish?

NAVY. That's fair enough. What do you change it to?

ARMY. Brook trout broiled with sliced almonds.

NAVY. Poached salmon with hollandaise sauce.

ARMY. *I thought you didn't like fish!!!*

NAVY. Maybe it's only the ones *you* like that I don't like.

ARMY. You're purposely doing this!

NAVY. You accuse me of being false to my taste?
. . . You dishonor me.

ARMY. I dishonor no one! . . . I call for a stalemate
on the fish.

NAVY. So soon? . . . Why give up? There are so
few fish that I like.

ARMY. Very well. . . . Filet of Sole cooked with
white wine and grapes.

NAVY. Sea Bass cooked in black bean sauce.

ARMY. *Stalemate!! . . . STALEMATE!!!*

NAVY. Don't get yourself so excited. We still have
a roast to get through. . . . Agreed. Stalemate. . . .

ARMY. (*Grumbling.*) . . . I don't understand why
there should be a stalemate when Pike is so delicious
. . . especially after we've just had borscht!

NAVY. What's past is past. . . . The table has been
cleared. . . . We're on the roast now. It's your turn.

ARMY. . . . I pass.

NAVY. You pass on the roast?

ARMY. I pass my *turn.* . . . I want *you* to go first.
I don't trust you anymore.

NAVY. It makes no difference to me. . . . For the
roast, I contend there is nothing better than boiled
beef served with white, hot horseradish, with giblets,
pearl onions, peas, beans, white bread and cold, spring
wine. . . . I can smell it now. I can barely contain
my mouth from dripping with saliva. . . . It is, I
believe, your turn, unless you concede to boiled beef.

ARMY. I do *not* concede to boiled beef.

NAVY. Then mention, if you can, a better roast.

ARMY. (*Pauses . . . thinks.*) . . . A nice piece of
Pike!

NAVY. *Pike is a fish!* . . . We're *through* with the
fish course!

ARMY. Not in the case of a stalemate. In a stalemate,
you can always go back and try again.

NAVY. When was this decided?

ARMY. Just now . . . *I* decided.

NAVY. Alright—if you say Pike again, I say brook trout again! . . . Double stalemate! . . . Next course! . . . Boiled beef! . . . *Your* turn!!

ARMY. (*With disgust.*) . . . Boiled Beef! . . . Herring, borscht and boiled beef. . . . It's a meal for a cold, hungry foot soldier, not a Commanding Officer and a gentleman.

NAVY. Am I being challenged or not?

ARMY. I could challenge boiled beef with a small partridge. I could challenge it with a brace of quail. I could challenge it with a firm, young *roast turkey*.

NAVY. (*Impressed.*) Roast turkey? . . . Hmmm . . . You may have something there.

ARMY. I could challenge your boiled beef with a hen, a fat, juicy, white meat, thick breasted *hen*. . . .

NAVY. I see what you mean. . . . A hen . . . Certainly . . . A hen is always nice.

ARMY. But I'm not going to do it. . . . I challenge boiled beef with a *duck!*

NAVY. A duck? . . . I didn't think of duck. . . . How did I overlook duck? . . . What kind of duck?

ARMY. A duckling. . . . A round, plump, young duckling . . . one that has had a taste of ice during the first frost . . . and then it's roasted . . . pan roasted to a crisp, golden brown . . . the skin so crisp that it *crackles* in your mouth. . . .

NAVY. I concede to duck!

ARMY. . . . roasted *with* the potatoes, cut small into the dripping pan—

NAVY. I *concede*, I said!

ARMY. —and the potatoes are turned and soaked in the duck fat, and in the pan, young onions are beginning to turn to a rich, deep brown, sizzling and frying in butter and fat, while the aroma wafts up into your nostrils driving your taste buds to a stage of frenzy—

NAVY. (*Screams.*) *How many times do I have to concede??* . . . Are you deaf?? . . . You're purposely

doing this to get back at me for not liking the Pike.
. . . I conceded to duck!! . . . Alright?? . . . The
main course is *over* with. . . . Now let's get to the
dessert. . . . For God sakes! . . .

ARMY. (*Softly.*) . . . and the duck is basking in the
juice of Spanish oranges. . . .

NAVY. *ENOUGH ALREADY!!!* . . . What's wrong
with you? . . . You're acting like a child over a silly
piece of Pike!

ARMY. *Try* it sometime, in butter and oil, you won't
think it's so silly.

NAVY. Do you want to continue or not?

ARMY. (*Reluctantly.*) Go ahead! . . . I'm still
savoring my duck.

NAVY. . . . For dessert. . . . I choose—

ARMY. Yes?

NAVY. I choose—for dessert. . . .

ARMY. Well? . . . Out with it! . . . If you can't
think of one, *I'll* choose.

NAVY. I'm thinking. . . . I want to end the perfect meal perfectly. . . . I chooooooooose—for des-
serrrrrrt. . . .

ARMY. (*Quickly.*) Cold peaches, sweet cream and
brandy!

NAVY. (*Angry.*) That's *mine!* . . . *I* choose peaches,
sweet cream and brandy! You can't take my dessert.

ARMY. I can take it if it takes you an hour to think
of it. . . . For a meal to be perfect, it's not only *what*
you eat, it's when it's *served!* . . . If I waited for you
to think of it, I would be hungry again. . . .

NAVY. I refuse to argue with you anymore.

ARMY. Then you concede the lunch?

NAVY. Are you through choosing?

ARMY. Certainly I'm through. . . . We've gone
through all the courses, haven't we? . . . The lunch
is over. . . . I've won a clear cut victory. . . . Concede the fact and we can go home.

NAVY. But you are definitely through choosing? As far as you're concerned, the lunch is over.

ARMY. Of course it's over. What in God's name could follow cold peaches, sweet cream and a brandy?

NAVY. (*Triumphant.*) A cigar. . . . A big, black panatella cigar. . . . Followed by a two hour nap.

ARMY. (*Gloomy.*) I forgot . . . I forgot a cigar and a nap.

NAVY. You know what kind of a nap you have after a good cigar? . . . Delicious. . . . A delicious nap. . . . It's not a hard working, tiring sleep like you have at night. . . . A light nap is delicate. . . . You sleep softly, with warm, sweet dreams like the kind you had when you were thirty. *That's* how you end the perfect lunch!

ARMY. How could I forget a cigar and a nap?

NAVY. And I'm not even through yet. . . . When you wake up, a mint. . . . A white, tangy peppermint, kills the entire sour taste in the mouth. . . .

ARMY. Alright. That's enough already. You've won, you don't have to rub my nose in it.

NAVY. And with the mint, the afternoon newspaper, a blanket on your lap, a cozy fire, and a dog at your feet to rub your toes on. . . . And as you sit there with your body warmed to a perfect temperature, you read only good news in the paper. . . . France is having political trouble, they're starving in Ireland, England is in a financial crisis . . . but here everything is good. . . . And just as you're about to fall off into the perfect sleep, a letter comes in the mail that the Czar has awarded you another medal. . . . And then you drop off with a smile on your face . . . the perfect lunch is over. . . . And you have nothing more to do until that evening . . . when the perfect dinner is served. . . . You want to challenge me for the perfect dinner? . . . I'll let you go first. . . . Hors d'oeuvres.

ARMY. It's my turn to choose the subject, not yours. . . .

NAVY. I've had enough for today. . . . I'm not feeling well. . . . A little chilly.

ARMY. You don't look so good. . . . A little pale. . . . Maybe you should see a doctor?

NAVY. It's a good idea. . . . Maybe I'll drop in on Doctor Vishinsky.

ARMY. Vishinsky? . . . That butcher? . . . He knows as much about doctoring as my three year old granddaughter.

NAVY. Are you trying to tell me you know a better doctor in Russia today than Vishinsky?

ARMY. Do you challenge me?

NAVY. I challenge you. . . . But not today. . . . Next week.

ARMY. Next week it is . . . (*He gets up, looks at sky.*) You're right. It *is* getting chilly.

NAVY. (*Gets up.*) No, I think it's beginning to warm up. Here comes the sun.

ARMY. It'll rain before you get home.

NAVY. Next Tuesday then?

ARMY. Next Tuesday.

(*They both turn and walk slowly off in the direction they entered from. The lights dim slowly . . . until we are in black.*)

CURTAIN

Tape Cues—The Good Doctor—Tape No. 1.*

The Concert

Oop Tymbali
Good Doctor Opus No. 1
Trans-Siberian Railroad
Father and Son
Good Doctor Opus No. 2
Gathering 1
Gathering 2

(End of Concert)

Act One
Scene 1. The Writer.

Cue 1. "It starts in a theatre" Cymbal sound.
Cue 2. "opening night of the new season" Cymbal.
Cue 3. "It starts"—tune up until "see that evening."
Cue 4. "one man . . . Ivan Ilyitch Cherdyakov!" until General sits.

Scene 2. The Sneeze.

Cue 5. Ta Da on "Lovely trees and bushes this year . . . Very nice. Ta Da.
Cue 6. Sneeze—drum roll as sneeze starts in the slow motion sequence.
Cue 7. on "No! I'm scared, Ivan."
Cue 8. from "Gibber, Gibber, Gibber" until "And yet—"
Cue 9. on "It is *he* who will be humiliated by *I*!"

*Tape cues especially prepared for Samuel French, Inc. by Stan Free.

85

Cue 10. on *"Nothing!!!"*

Cue 11. Finale from "for all, forever. . . ." until "died!"

Scene 3. The Governess.

Cue 12. on "But some of us are indeed, trapped."

Cue 13. from "Yes M'am . . . it's possible." until "Wait!"

Scene 4. Surgery.

Cue 14. from "in the village of Astemko," until "an inexperienced one."

End of Tape No. 1.

Tape No. 2.

Cue 1. Crossover from Scene 4 from "Hail Mary! Hail Mary!" until "Good afternoon, Madame."

Scene 5. Too Late for Happiness.

Note: First take on song is for rehearsal, second take is a track without vocal—the entire scene is underscored.

Scene 6. The Seduction.

Cue 2. from "through the *husband*. . . ." until "approaches."

Cue 3. from "How soon will she be mine?" until "I saw Peter Semyonych today . . ."

Cue 4. on "weakening, weakening."

Cue 5. from "She ran all the way." until "after all, a gentleman."

Cue 6. on "his lovely young wife."

Entr'acte

Act Two

Scene 1. The Drowned Man.

Cue 7. from "distant ships" until "a little night air to clear my mind."

Cue 8. from "what was that fellow's name?" until "Next actress, please!"

Scene 2. The Audition.

Cue 9. from "back to Odessa. . . ." until "enters."

Scene 3. A Defenseless Creature.

Cue 10. on "she's coming back. . . ."

Scene 4. The Arrangement.

Cue 11. from "Yes Poppa." until "stage dims out."

Scene 5. The Writer.

Cue 12. from "Good night." through exit and bows— 2 takes.

End of Tape No. 2.

COSTUME PLOT

ACT ONE

"THE WRITER"

Narrator—Off-white silk shirt with large white satin tie-bow, off-white moire vest, dark navy blue Russian wool overcoat, black corduroy Russian cap, black boots gold pince nez, gold pocket watch and chain.

"THE SNEEZE"

Narrator—Same as in "The Writer" except for black velvet frock coat and white gloves.

Cherdyakov—Dark green velvet cutaway coat, gray and black striped trousers, blue and white striped shirt with a white collar, parchment colored vest with gray figures, ragged gray short wool coat and gray wool neck scarf, black boots, white bow tie, yellow hanky in pocket, pair of glasses.

General—White shirt with tie stock collar, black trousers with double black braid stripe, black wool tunic piped in red with gold and white collar and epaulets, red grosgrain sash with gold stripes, braided gold tassels, medals, black sword belt with silver sword, black high boots worn over trousers, white gloves, white handkerchief.

Madame Brassilhov—Black taffeta waist petticoat, black velvet long dress with high neck and slight train trimmed with fake chinchilla and black beading, moire black velvet short cape embroidered with silver and jet black pineapples, red ribbon, red ribbon trimming on shoulders of cape, black fur hat with black velvet and red moire taffeta trim, silver pin and spikey feathers on hat, black lace gloves and beaded black reticule, black boots.

Wife—White eyelet skirt, ankle-length trimmed with red and white stripes. Red crushed velvet jacket with lace collar and trim down the front, pin, red bow on back of skirt, red velvet matching beret, white gloves, black ankle boots, white reticule, gold dressing gown with tie belt worn over long white petticoat.

"THE GOVERNESS"

Mistress—Blue velvet long dress with high neck, long sleeves and slight train, pin with artificial flowers, black boots.

Julia—Long black skirt, white dotted swiss blouse with high neck and long sleeves, white crocheted short jacket, black boots.

"SURGERY"

Narrator—Black and white check trousers, black and white tweed vest, black woolen "Writers" coat.

Kuryatin—Same trousers and vest as the Narrator, dirty white dentist coat, kneelength with half-belt and mandarin collar, dirty white Russian cap.

Sexton—Brown cassock-like robe with peasant sash and crucifix, brown fez-shaped cap, dark red bloomer trousers, short black Russian boots worn over trousers, red beard.

"TOO LATE FOR HAPPINESS"

Man—Brown check coat trimmed with fur collar and cuffs, bloomer pants from "Surgery," red wool neck scarf, brown corduroy Russian cap and short black boots.

Woman—Beige coat (mid-calf), skirt attached to coat, matching beige hat with feather trim, brown leather gloves, brown cloth purse.

"THE SEDUCTION"

Narrator—Black woolen "Writers" coat worn over white suit, pince-nez.

Peter Smyonych—Off-white silk shirt, white silk suit with cutaway coat, white bow tie, large white fedora, white boots, white cane.

Husband—White on white figured shirt, white vest, pale gray and white wool tweed trousers, pale gray frock coat, pale gray derby, long-john underwear cut off at knees with Dr. Denton flap in back, white boots, pale gray cravat.

Wife—Long white dress with high neck and long sleeves, slight train and ice-blue belt, white hat with white lace trim, white petticoat with eyelet trim, white chemise top, white boots, white pumps, white reticule, white parasol, white lacy floor-length negligee with hood.

ACT II

"THE DROWNED MAN"

Narrator—Gray and black stripe trousers, gray and black stripe vest, gray flannel cutaway coat, dark gray tweed cape coat, black top hat, black boots, gray cravat.

Sailor—Battered brown herringbone tweed trousers, leather jerkin, dirty gray wool short coat, dirty brown long wool neck scarf, beat up gray stripe cravat, beat up brown derby, black boots, brown wool gloves with fingers cut off.

Policeman—Dark green (almost black) policeman's overcoat with red epaulets and gold braid on each sleeve, gold buttons, high boots, sword belt with black sword, black leather gloves, black policeman's helmet trimmed with an eagle on the front.

"THE AUDITION"

Girl—Blue cotton blouse with high neck and long sleeves, beige ankle-length skirt, white wool knit long jacket with red embroidery, red scarf with hood and white lace trim, multi-colored small carpetbag, black boots.

"A DEFENSELESS CREATURE"

Assistant—Gray and black stripe trousers, gray silk shirt with white collar and cuffs, off-white vest, dark gray cutaway coat with white handkerchief, black gaiter boots, two-tone gray cravat.

Kistunov—Same ensemble as in "The Drowned Man" except without cape coat and top hat. Large white foot cast.

Woman—Rust colored Russian peasant shirt, ankle-length quilted patchwork skirt, rust colored shawl with black fringe, red kerchief on head, rust colored sack-purse.

"THE ARRANGEMENT"

Narrator—Same ensemble as "Drowned Man" except without cape coat or cutaway coat.

Father—Same as Narrator except he wears "Writers" coat, top hat.

Son—Off-white stripe shirt, black and white small check trousers, rusty brown cravat, black frock coat, black gaiter boots, black Russian cap.

Girl—Black coat with sequined collar and cuffs, eggplant colored boa, black hat trimmed with black and purple ostrich feathers and sequins, red wig, purple velvet reticule, black gloves.

"THE WRITER"

Narrator—Same ensemble as in "The Arrangement" except without top hat.

PROPERTY PLOT

ACT ONE

PRE-SET:
  On Stage Center:
    "Writer's Desk" (1—1)
    On it:
      Real rose (red) in vase (1—1)
    In drawer:
      10 silver coins (1—3)
      1 brown envelope (1—3)
    In bin:
      Dental forceps (1—4)
  On Stage Right Center:
    "Writer's Bench" (no back) (1—1)
On Stage Left Unit:
    Mushroom stool (1—4)
Off Stage Left Unit:
    "General's Desk" (1—2)
On Stage Right Unit:
    Square stool (1—4)
    On Peg:
      Black velvet coat (wardrobe)
Off Stage Right Unit:
    Icons (on shelf)
    On Peg:
      Gray cloth coat and scarf (wardrobe)
Off Stage Right:
    Small round stool (2—2)
    "Seduction Bench" with back (1—6)
    Low arm chair (1—3)
    Crutch (2—2)
Off Stage Left:
    Box with rope handles (2—1)

PROP LIST

1 red rose—(real)
1 15 x 20 leather portfolio
6 sheets parchment with writing

1 small silver pen
1 Pin-Nez eyeglasses
5 red theatre programs with ribbon
1 small round straw box of choc. candy
1 lorgnette-tortoise shell
1 silver dental mirror
1 pair large scissor
1 plastic tipped forceps
Cigars
Stick matches
1 pair men's round silver rimmed eyeglasses
1 8½ x 11 leather ledger and pen
1 pair woman's round silver rimmed eyeglasses
1 small brown leather book and marker strip
1 knotted wood walking stick
1 gray silver handled walking stick
1 silver handled black walking stick
1 white silver handled walking stick
1 small marbleized pocket notebook and pen
1 Russian newspaper
Large silver coins (10)
Small white calling cards
Small round bottle medicine (with red food coloring)
1 spoon
1 multi-colored cloth shopping bag
1 bunch celery
1 bunch turnips
1 doctor's certificate
1 pair gold rimmed eyeglasses
3 wooden icons
5 to 10 large gold-edged ledgers
1 silver desk bell
1 red corduroy cushion with trim
1 square crate with rope handles
1 low wood arm chair
3 assorted stools—wood
1 wooden bench with back
1 wooden bench—no back
1 desk on casters with detachable bench & 1 drawer
1 desk
Fairy dust

ACT ONE

Down Stage Left:
    "Teeth Book" (1—4)
In One Down Left:
    Metal rack
    On it:
        Dentist cap (1—5) (wardrobe)
        *Dentist coat (1—5) (wardrobe)
*PRESET IN DENTIST COAT: (1—5)
    Left Pocket:
        Stick matches (3 or 4)
        Cigar
    Right Pocket:
        Scissors
        Dental mirror

ACT ONE

During (1—2) (*"The Sneeze"*)
  After unit revolve and during first B.O. stage right
    Stage Right—STRIKE:
        "Writer's Bench" *Off*
Black Out (1—2) (*"The Sneeze"*)
    Stage Right—SET:
        Low arm chair
Black Out (1—3) (*"The Governess"*)
    Stage Left—STRIKE:
        "General's Desk"
    THEN—*Stage Left:*
        Clothes rack *On* (when actor approaches left)
        Clothes rack *Off* (when actor exits away)
Black Out (1—3) (*"The Governess"*)
    Stage Right—SET:
        Up Stage—Behind Drop
        "Seduction Bench" (with back) (1—6)
        On it:
            White hat and cane
        "Writer's Bench" (1—5)
Black Out (1—4) (*"Surgery"*)
    Stage Right—STRIKE:
        Low arm chair and stool

SET:
 Move "Writer's Bench" D.S.C. to marks
 Stage Left—STRIKE:
 "Writer's Desk" and Teeth Book
During (1—5) (*"Too Late for Happiness"*):
 Stage Left—SET:
 Mattress on Bed—*Off Left* unit
Black Out (1—5) (*"Too Late for Happiness"*):
 Stage Left—STRIKE:
 "Writer's Bench" (no back) to *Off Right*

ACT TWO

Intermission—STRIKE and PRESET:
STRIKE:
 On Stage:
 "Seduction Bench"
 Left Stage Unit:
 Bedding and newspaper
 Off Stage Left:
 "Writer's" Portfolio from behind *"Writer's Desk"*
PRESET:
 On Stage Left of Dock:
 Box with rope handles
 On Stage Left Unit:
 Mushroom stool (Dressing)
 Off Stage Right Unit:
 "General's Desk"

 On it:
 Bell
 Low arm chair with red cushion
 Square stool
 Small round stool
 Ledgers and books and one Icon on shelf
 Off Stage Right:
 (S.M.) Set microphone, "Audition" pages and
 turn on clip lite
 Off Stage Left:
 Black leather cap on desk

ACT TWO

Black Out (2—1) (*"Drowned Man"*)
>*Stage Left*—STRIKE:
>>Box with rope handles

End (2—2) (*"The Audition"*)
>*Stage Right*—SET:
>>Position *low arm chair* as unit revolves (2—3)

>*Stage Left:*
>>Add top hat and cane on "Writer's Desk"
>>to black leather cap (2—4)

Black Out (2—3) (*"A Defenseless Creature"*)
>*Stage Right*—STRIKE:
>>Small round stool as unit revolves

>*Stage Left*—SET:
>>"Writer's Portfolio" on U.S. platform

ACT ONE

1. THE WRITER:
>Writer's portfolio (Writer)
>Pin-nez eyeglasses (Writer)

2. THE SNEEZE:
>3 red theatre programs (Wife)
>1 round straw box candy (Wife)
>1 red theatre program (Mdme Brassilov)
>1 red theatre program (General)
>Silver rimmed eyeglasses (Cherdyakov)
>Small pocket notebook (General)

3. THE GOVERNESS:
>1 leather ledger and pen (Mistress)
>Silver rimmed eyeglasses (Governess)

5. "TOO LATE FOR HAPPINESS"
>Small brown book (Old Woman)
>Knotted walking stick (Old Man)

6. THE SEDUCTION:
>Silver handled black cane (Narrator)
>Silver handled gray cane (Husband)
>Small pocket noteboob and pen (Husband)

ACT TWO

1. THE DROWNED MAN:
   Silver Coins (Narrator)
   Cigar (Sailor)
   Small white card (Police Officer)

3. THE DEFENSELESS CREATURE:
   Small round bottle medicine (Pochatkin)
   1 spoon (Pochatkin)
   Cloth shipping bag (Woman)
   Doctor's certificate (Woman)
   Square gold rimmed eyeglasses (Kistunov)

4. THE ARRANGEMENT:
   Silver coins (Father)

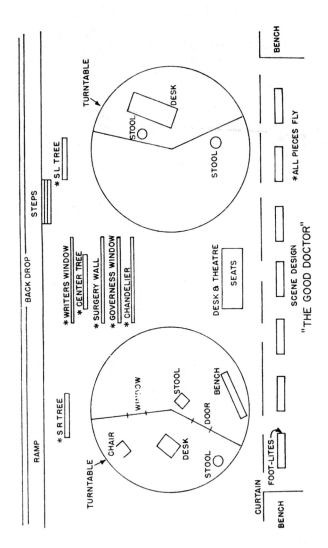

SCENE DESIGN
"THE GOOD DOCTOR"

98

Come Blow Your Horn

By NEIL SIMON

COMEDY

3 men, 4 women—Interior

This fresh and delightful comedy was the surprise hit of the recent New York season. Harry Baker, owner of the largest artificial fruit business in the east, is the father of two sons. One is a 33-year-old playboy; the other a different, 21-year-old with an urge to assert himself. These two are continually trying their father's easily abused patience. Alan works only two days a week and goes on skiing or golfing jaunts with attractive female companions the other five. Buddy, hitherto an obedient son who even kissed Aunt Gussie through her veil at Dad's request, has moved into Alan's apartment, leaving a rebellious letter by way of explanation. The richly comic complications that ensue are unfailingly inventive and arise out of character, are never mere gags. "A slick, lively, funny comedy."—*N. Y. Times.* "It's completely nuts and banging with laughs."—*N. Y. World-Telegram & Sun.* "Warm-hearted and amusing."—*N. Y. Daily News.*

A Thousand Clowns

By HERB GARDNER

COMEDY

4 men, 1 woman, 1 boy 12 years old—2 interiors

Having created America's funniest creatures, the Nebishes, Herb Gardner turned his sights on Broadway and created the funniest play of the season, with "A Thousand Clowns." Jason Robards, Jr., opened in the role of a bachelor uncle who had been left to rear his precocious nephew. He has tired of writing cheap comedy for a children's television program, and now finds himself unemployed. But he also finds he has the free time to saunter through New York and do everything he has always wanted—like standing on Park Avenue in the dawn's early light and hollering, "All right, all you rich people: everybody out in the street for volleyball." This is not the right upbringing for a boy, however, and so a social service team comes to investigate him. Soon, however, he is solving their problems for them. He has to go back to work, or lose his nephew. Then on the other hand, he might even marry the girl social worker. The only thing we're certain of is that he will always be a cheerful non-conformist of the first rank.

The Gingerbread Lady

NEIL SIMON
(Little Theatre) Comedy-Drama
3 Men, 3 Women—Interior

Maureen Stapleton played the Broadway part of a popular singer who has gone to pot with booze and sex. We meet her at the end of a ten-week drying out period at a sanitarium, when her friend, her daughter, and an actor try to help her adjust to sobriety. But all three have the opposite effect on her. The friend is so constantly vain she loses her husband; the actor, a homosexual, is also doomed, and indeed loses his part three days before an opening; and the daughter needs more affection than she can spare her mother. Enter also a former lover louse, who ends up giving her a black eye. The birthday party washes out, the gingerbread lady falls off the wagon and careens onward to her own tragic end.

> "He has combined an amusing comedy with the atmosphere of great sadness. His characteristic wit and humor are at their brilliant best, and his serious story of lost misfits can often be genuinely and deeply touching."—N.Y. Post. "Contains some of the brightest dialogue Simon has yet composed."—N.Y. Daily News. "Mr. Simon's play is as funny as ever—the customary avalanche of hilarity, and landslide of pure unbuttoned joy . . . Mr. Simon is a funny, funny man—with tears running down his cheek."—N.Y. Times.

The Sunshine Boys

NEIL SIMON
(All Groups) Comedy
5 Men, 2 Women

An ex-vaudeville team, Al Lewis and Willie Clarke, in spite of playing together for forty-three years, have a natural antipathy for one another. (Willie resents Al's habit of poking a finger in his chest, or perhaps accidentally spitting in his face). It has been eleven years since they have performed together, when along comes CBS-TV, who is preparing a "History of Comedy" special, that will of course include Willie and Al—the "Lewis and Clark" team back together again. In the meantime, Willie has been doing spot commercials, like for Schick (the razor blade shakes) or for Frito-Lay potato chips (he forgets the name), while Al is happily retired. The team gets back together again, only to have Al poke his finger in Willie's chest, and accidentally spit in his face.

> ". . . the most delightful play Mr. Simon has written for several seasons and proves why he is the ablest current author of stage humor."—Watts, N. Y. Post. "None of Simon's comedies has been more intimately written out of love and a bone-deep affinity with the theatrical scene and temperament." Time. ". . . another hit for Neil Simon in this shrewdly balanced, splendidly performed and rather touching slice of the show-biz life."—Watt, New York Daily News. "(Simon) . . . writes the most dependably crisp and funny dialogue around . . . always well-set and polished to a high lustre."—WABC-TV. ". . . a vaudeville act within a vaudeville act . . . Simon has done it again."—WCBS-TV.

DON'T DRINK THE WATER

By WOODY ALLEN

FARCE

12 men, 4 women—Interior

A CASCADE OF COMEDY FROM ONE OF OUR FUNNIEST CO-MEDIANS, and a solid hit on Broadway, this affair takes place inside an American embassy behind the Iron Curtain. An American tourist, caterer by trade, and his family of wife and daughter rush into the embassy two steps ahead of the police, who suspect them of spying and picture-taking. But it's not much of a refuge, for the ambassador is absent and his son, now in charge, has been expelled from a dozen countries and the whole continent of Africa. Nevertheless, they carefully and frantically plot their escape, and the ambassador's son and the caterer's daughter even have time to fall in love. "Because Mr. Allen is a working comedian himself, a number of the lines are perfectly agreeable . . . and there's quite a delectable bit of business laid out by the author and manically elaborated by the actor. . . . The gag is pleasantly outrageous and impeccably performed."—*N. Y. Times.* "Moved the audience to great laughter. . . . Allen's imagination is daffy, his sense of the ridiculous is keen and gags snap, crackle and pop."—*N. Y. Daily News.* "It's filled with funny lines. . . . A master of bright and hilarious dialogue."—*N. Y. Post.*

THE ODD COUPLE

By NEIL SIMON

COMEDY

6 men, 2 women—Interior

NEIL SIMON'S THIRD SUCCESS in a row begins with a group of the boys assembled for cards in the apartment of a divorced fellow, and if the mess of the place is any indication, it's no wonder that his wife left him. Late to arrive is another fellow who, they learn, has just been separated from his wife. Since he is very meticulous and tense, they fear he might commit suicide, and so go about locking all the windows. When he arrives, he is scarcely allowed to go to the bathroom alone. As life would have it, the slob bachelor and the meticulous fellow decide to bunk together—with hilarious results. The patterns of their own disastrous marriages begin to reappear in this arrangement; and so this too must end. "The richest comedy Simon has written and purest gold for any theatregoer. . . . This glorious play."—*N. Y. World-Telegram & Sun.* "His skill is not only great but constantly growing. . . . There is scarcely a moment that is not hilarious."—*N. Y. Times.*

Other Publications for Your Interest

THE WHITE HOUSE MURDER CASE
(LITTLE THEATRE—MORALITY)
By JULES FEIFFER

9 men, 1 woman—Interior, interior inset.

The incisive satire of Jules Feiffer is here aimed at the war posture of the United States in some future time. The war this year is in Brazil, and the American poison gas attack backfires. The President is worried about what to tell the people on the eve of an election, how to explain the gas being in the "U.S. peace arsenal." A staunch old general, blinded and crippled by war, comes in and demonstrates by his stoicism the idiocy of outmoded codes. While the cabinet is concocting a cock-and-bull story for the people, the President's wife is murdered. The duplicity of the President then comes to the fore: "The crime must be solved and then an explanation for the United States people readied." In lieu of film strips of the war, there are life-size scenes, showing a C.I.A. man rescuing a foot soldier, and then the two of them getting to know one another—before they kill each other. "A very funny, very savage man. He takes a man-sized swipe at our modern society. There is so much that is brilliant in the conception of The White House Murder Case."—N.Y. Times. "Tremendously funny. A witty, wonderful comedy."—WCBS-TV.

ROMANTIC COMEDY
(LITTLE THEATRE—COMEDY)
By BERNARD SLADE

2 men, 4 women—Interior

Arrogant, self-centered and sharp-tongued Jason Carmichael, successful coauthor of Broadway romantic comedies is facing two momentous events; he's about to marry a society belle and his collaborator is retiring from the fray. Enter Phoebe Craddock, mousy Vermont schoolteacher and budding playwright, Presto! Jason acquires a talented and adoring collaborator. Fame and success are theirs for ten years and then Jason's world falls apart. His wife divorces him to go into politics (says Jason, "I married Grace Kelly and wound up with Bella Abzug")—and Phoebe, her love for Jason unrequited, marries a breezy journalist and moves to Paris. Jason goes into professional, financial and physical decline. Reenter a now chic and successful-in-her-own-right Phoebe—and guess the ending! Meaty roles for the supporting cast. Starred Tony Perkins and Mia Farrow on Broadway. "A darling of a play . . . zesty entertainment of cool wit and warm sentiment."—N.Y. Post. "An utterly disarming, lighthearted confection about love, friendship and theatrical trauma."—WWD. "It's brilliant comedy. It's also a hit. Funniest comedy on Broadway in years."—WABC-TV7. "Marvelously entertaining . . . very funny and touching."—WCBS-TV2.

Other Publications for Your Interest

I'M NOT RAPPAPORT
(LITTLE THEATRE—COMEDY)
By HERB GARDNER

5 men, 2 women—Exterior

Just when we thought there would never be another joyous, laugh-filled evening on Broadway, along came this delightful play to restore our faith in the Great White Way. If you thought *A Thousand Clowns* was wonderful, wait til you take a look at *I'm Not Rappaport!* Set in a secluded spot in New York's Central Park, the play is about two octogenarians determined to fight off all attempts to put them out to pasture. Talk about an odd couple! Nat is a lifelong radical determined to fight injustice (real or imagined) who is also something of a spinner of fantasies. He has a delightful repertoire of eccentric personas, which makes the role an actor's dream. The other half of this unlikely partnership is Midge, a Black apartment super who spends his days in the park hiding out from tenants, who want him to retire. "Rambunctiously funny."—N.Y. Post. "A warm and entertaining evening."—W.W. Daily. **Tony Award Winner, Best Play 1986. Posters.**

(#11071)

CROSSING DELANCEY
(LITTLE THEATRE—COMEDY)
By SUSAN SANDLER

2 men, 3 women—Comb. Interior/Exterior.

Isabel is a young Jewish woman who lives alone and works in a NYC bookshop. When she is not pining after a handsome author who is one of her best customers, she is visiting her grandmother—who lives by herself in the "old neighborhood", Manhattan's Lower East Side. Isabel is in no hurry to get married, which worries her grandmother. The delightfully nosey old lady hires an old friend who is—can you believe this in the 1980's?—a matchmaker. Bubbie and the matchmaker come up with a Good Catch for their Isabel—Sam, a young pickle vendor. Same is no *schlemiel*, though. He likes Isabel; but he knows he is going to have to woo her, which he proceeds to do. When Isabel realizes what a cad the author is, and what a really nice man Sam is, she begins to respond; and the end of the play is really a beginning, ripe with possibilities for Isabel and "An amusing interlude for theatregoers who may have thought that simple romance and sentimentality had long since been relegated to television sitcoms...tells its unpretentious story believeably, rarely trying to make its gag lines, of which there are many, upstage its narration or outshine its heart."—N.Y. Times. "A warm and loving drama...a welcome addition to the growing body of Jewish dramatic work in this country."—Jewish Post and Opinion.

(#5739)

Other Publications for Your Interest

NOISES OFF
(LITTLE THEATRE—FARCE)

By MICHAEL FRAYN

5 men, 4 women—2 Interiors

This wonderful Broadway smash hit is "a farce about farce, taking the cliches of the genre and shaking them inventively through a series of kaleidoscopic patterns. Never missing a trick, it has as its first act a pastiche of traditional farce; as its second, a contemporary variant on the formula; as its third, an elaborate undermining of it. The play opens with a touring company dress-rehearsing 'Nothing On', a conventional farce. Mixing mockery and homage, Frayn heaps into this play-within-a-play a hilarious melee of stock characters and situations. Caricatures—cheery char, outraged wife and squeaky blonde—stampede in and out of doors. Voices rise and trousers fall . . . a farce that makes you think as well as laugh."—London Times Literary Supplement. ". . . as side-splitting a farce as I have seen. Ever? *Ever*."—John Simon, NY Magazine. "The term 'hilarious' must have been coined in the expectation that something on the order of this farce-within-a-farce would eventually come along to justify it."—N.Y. Daily News. "Pure fun."—N.Y. Post. "A joyous and loving reminder that the theatre really does go on, even when the show falls apart."—N.Y. Times.   (#16052)

THE REAL THING
(ADVANCED GROUPS—COMEDY)

By TOM STOPPARD

4 men, 3 women—Various settings

The effervescent Mr. Stoppard has never been more intellectually—and *emotionally*—engaging than in this "backstage" comedy about a famous playwright named Henry Boot whose second wife, played on Broadway to great acclaim by Glenn Close (who won the Tony Award), is trying to merge "worthy causes" (generally a euphemism for left-wing politics) with her art as an actress. She has met a "political prisoner" named Brodie who has been jailed for radical thuggery, and who has written an inept play about how property is theft, about how the State stifles the Rights of The Individual, etc., etc., etc. Henry's wife wants him to make the play work theatrically, which he does after much soul-searching. Eventually, though, he is able to convince his wife that Brodie is emphatically *not* a victim of political repression. He is, in fact, a *thug*. Famed British actor Jeremy Irons triumphed in the Broadway production (Tony Award), which was directed to perfection by none other than Mike Nichols (Tony Award). "So densely and entertainingly packed with wit, ideas and feelings that one visit just won't do . . . Tom Stoppard's most moving play and the most bracing play anyone has written about love and marriage in years."—N.Y. Times. "Shimmering, dazzling theatre, a play of uncommon wit and intelligence which not only thoroughly delights but challenges and illuminates our lives."—WCBS-TV. 1984 Tony Award-Best Play.   (#941)